Pimpernel

Starbreaker

Pimpernel
Starbreaker

SHERALYN PRATT

Cover Design: Sheralyn Pratt

ISBN : 9781795005128

First Published, January 2019
on the "Super Blood Wolf Moon"

Wicked Sassy, LLC
Salt Lake City, Utah

10 9 8 7 6 5 4 3 2 1

I'm a slave for you.
I cannot hold it;
I cannot control it.
I'm a slave for you.
I won't deny it;
I'm not trying to hide it.

—I'm a Slave 4 U

Chapter 1

Taking one final measurement across the cedar board, Jack penciled in a V to mark the cut line for the final shelf of a bookcase. Then he made the cut.

The bookcase was for Claire from a design he'd found pinned on her Pinterest page. The blueprints for it had all but drawn themselves once Jack combined her notes with the pictured design.

He was building it as a welcome-home gift—a day that was still a ways off.

Technically, Claire had only been gone thirty-nine days.

It felt longer.

Over the years, Jack had grown used to intermittent contact with the people he cared about most. He saw his parents two or three times a year, and only met up with his brother when there was a win-win to be had between them.

Jack was familiar with the sensation of missing people often and had known he would miss Claire while she was at her internship. He just didn't realize how much ... or how specifically.

He missed her voice, for one. Gentle, thoughtful, insightful, and sometimes a little manic.

For the past year, he'd had Claire in his ear daily—no matter where he was in the world—helping him see whatever he was facing in a new light. Where most people got overwhelmed, she grew focused until she found elegant solutions to seemingly insurmountable problems.

There was a symbiosis he felt with Claire that he'd never felt with anyone before.

Jack and Margot were like a pair of shoes when it came to working together—right-left, right-left. They knew each other's paces and limits, pushing and checking when they needed to. Their dynamic came from a lifetime of friendship and years working side-by-side.

He and Claire didn't pace like that. They had something better ... something Jack found himself missing more and more each day.

And missing her was turning itself into a bookcase for her new workspace—barn doors over the center two shelves with display shelves off to the side. It was a better way to spend his time than staring at his phone and trying to find justification to get Claire on the line somehow.

It wasn't allowed.

He knew that.

It was Claire's time to learn, to define her gift, and to decide how she wanted to use it. Boyfriends and "I miss you" calls were a distraction.

The best way to support Claire now was to use the time and the angst to make preparations for her return.

When Jack was done building her dream bookcase, he'd find something else to build, and keep repeating the pattern until six months had passed.

Only 141 days left to go.

But it was better to count measurements than days. So Jack kept measuring and cutting until he had sixteen shelves of uniform length stacked and ready for sanding.

Out of habit, he pulled out a broom and cleaned up the sawdust from the cuts. His mentor had been a stickler about cleaning between phases of labor, and the old-school habit had stuck.

Who knew that habit would be one of the qualities that helped him get the girl in the end? Claire did like things tidy.

He was vacuuming the gathered dust when Margot's voice spoke in his ear.

"Are you at a stopping point?" she asked.

Jack turned off the vacuum. "Yep. What's up?"

"We have a visitor with a proposal for you."

"On my way," Jack said, finishing the vacuum job and heading to the elevator as he wondered about the word *proposal.*

He couldn't remember Margot using that word before.

Assignment? Yes. Job? Yes.

Proposal? What was that supposed to mean?

He was about to find out.

The elevator opened automatically as Jack approached, auto-selecting the correct floor for him and escorting him up as he inspected his clothes for dust. He was a bit underdressed for an official meeting, but this didn't sound official.

It sounded like a favor.

When the doors opened again on the far side of Margot's office, Jack stepped in and immediately recognized the signature bright smile and carefree curls of one of the most successful "psychics" in the world.

Wanda Amar.

The woman sat in one of Margot's guest chairs like she owned the place. But that was Wanda—always the biggest personality in the room.

Cupids often were.

Part of their job description was the ability to hold the full attention of a room at any time, in any place, working their magic with a persona that made their successes look like dumb luck.

Wanda definitely pulled off that feat to perfection. Her black curls were teased out, framing flawless chocolate skin and perfect teeth. Her heels and slacks were matching shades of tan that were all business, contrasting with a top that looked like a candy-store explosion. It paired nicely with her many bracelets and the oversized diamond on her ring finger.

The diamond solitaire could not be missed and perfectly advertised how much trouble a man would find himself in if he decided to pretend not to see it.

Jack had met Wanda's husband, Titus, just once. The man was a beast on two legs.

To call Wanda and Titus a power couple would be a vast understatement. They were both rated exceptional in their chosen fields which begged the question: Why would Wanda ever come looking Jack's way for help?

"A Cupid in a Royal's office?" he said, walking toward her. "Well, this isn't a sight I ever expected to see."

"I know, right?" Wanda said with her usual verve.

Her eyes seemed to track behind him as if expecting someone else to join them. When she saw nothing, she did one of her signature Wanda moves, blinking a little too long to get a read on the room as she chose her next words. "So let's jump to the part where I confess that my being here isn't strictly on the up-and-up."

Jack looked Margot's way to see how she was taking the confession and found his business partner maintaining her usual Royal visage.

He refocused on Wanda, taking the seat across from her. "Why would this not be on the up-and-up?"

Wanda's expression became the model of innocence as she confessed, "Technically speaking, I may have a bet riding on the outcome of what I'm here to talk to you about."

That was to be expected. "How much?"

Wide-eyed innocence was replaced with a frown. "Fifty coin."

That got both of Jack's eyebrows up. "Fifty coin?"

That was fifty markers good for fifty no-questions-asked favors.

From a Cupid to whoever bet against her.

4

That was bad.

Wanda waved what he could only call jazz hands of innocence his way. "In my defense, I didn't bet on this event, in particular. Cupids bet on love, not murder. But one of the lovers I bet on is about to be assassinated, and I think we can both admit that's not fair. I bet on two soulmates finding a way to overcome the obstacles between them in this crazy world. And I stand by my bet. If my soulmates spend even a day together, they'll be married within a year. Anyone can bet fifty coin on that all day long—so long as no one calls in a hitman."

That all made sense, but it didn't explain why Wanda was sitting in front of him. "So why not save them yourself? Forfeit your bet and save the day."

"Can't," she said with a pout. "Terms say I'd have to pay out in full to everyone in the pool—including eight fae—if I bail. And I think we all know what a disaster that would be."

Disaster was an understatement. Four hundred no-questions-asked favors in the fae's hands from one of the most skilled potion-makers on the planet?

Jack didn't want to know what kind of chaos that might bring.

"And all the charts I can think to make say there wouldn't be a point anyway," Wanda continued, looking more than a little grumpy about it. "Everything says the assassin will win—even with Titus on the scene, if you can believe it. And my baby has never lost an asset."

Ah, astrology. Jack's least favorite predictive filter on the planet. He never used it. Ever. Hated it, in fact. But it was a favorite in the House of Hearts. And once a chart spoke, they believed with unquestioning faith. There was no talking logic into a Heart once a chart had spoken.

"So why come to me?" he asked, praying her answer wouldn't be some nonsense about a prophetic horoscope. The answer he got was almost worse.

"A fae contingency bet."

5

Great. That boded well.

"If you check out the betting pools on the Good Ship Nemo," she continued, "it's me against the world when it comes to this bet. But there is one fae betting my way if Cobalt and his Shade show up to save the day."

Jack could only think of one fae who would make that bet. Tiki … a known associate of Malachi.

Had Malachi directed Tiki to make the bet, or was Tiki still fangirling like Kali was a one-woman boy band?

There was no way to know for sure but it did raise Jack's curiosity about the intended target.

"I must confess," Wanda said like a friend gossiping over lunch. "I was a bit surprised to learn you had a Shade these days. But once I learned that was true, I had to swing by. I mean, I may not be able to hire you or ask you to interfere, but there are no rules against me gossiping a bit as I swing through town. And if you hear something that interests you, then you're free to do whatever you want from there. Right?"

Jack had to give it to her. The woman was sly. Jack was always interested in saving a life, but there was a problem.

"What would be my motive for taking on the case?" he asked. "Certainly no one is going to believe I plucked this particular case up at random."

Wanda and Margot shared a look then—Wanda looking eagerly Margot's way and Margot responding with a regal nod.

The next time Wanda met Jack's eyes, she had the look of a woman who knew she was about to win. "Because there is another player in the game that I think you want to catch."

Jack kept his face unreadable. "And who might that be?"

Wanda's look turned solemn. "Someone hired Ceravene."

Jack felt his heart hammer in his chest. No way a man like him would advertise a target in advance.

"Ceravene? Are you sure?"

She nodded. "It's why so many are betting against me. One fae let it drop that there's a Starbreaker on the other side who has been hired to ensure one of my soulmates ceases to be by the new moon, and everyone dogpiled on from there."

Jack could tell they'd reached the point in the discussion where Margot had called him in because she knew he'd want this case.

He did. Without question.

Just like he knew Margot couldn't assist him in any planning or execution. Considering the target, all Royal assets would be withheld from him if he agreed to this venture. It really would be him and Kali.

But he was in. All he needed to do was get Kali onboard.

"Where is this all happening?" he asked.

"Los Angeles," Wanda replied, and Jack felt his stomach sink a little.

Kali's old stomping grounds. She had a lot of history there ... a lot of memories.

Was it too soon to force her back?

He was about to find out.

"Give me thirty minutes," he replied, standing from his seat. "Then let's meet back here and you can tell me what you know about the situation."

Wanda sent him a sly smile. "Mmhmm, honey. I'll go make the tea."

Chapter 2

Watching from the edge of the room as Ren and Kali sparred, Jack had to confess Kali's skill levels were becoming a bit spooky.

When Jack had first crossed paths with her a few years ago, Kali had been promising. But the potential he'd seen in her had long since been surpassed.

The pint-sized woman was all but superhuman now.

Gravity seemed optional in Kali's movements. Her spatial awareness was unreal—allowing for effortless mid-air adjustments that Jack wouldn't even think to attempt with a safety net. But Kali somehow always found her feet when it was time for her and the ground to meet. In a split second, she could turn an impossible landing into a seamless one.

Jack had never seen anything quite like it and he was pretty sure Ren hadn't either.

The two of them often trained together. Sparring with Ren put Kali at a nearly hundred-pound and an eighteen-inch-reach disadvantage. Statistically speaking, Ren had every advantage in a face-off, but Jack hadn't seen any of those statistics result in more landed strikes since they'd started training together.

In fact, Ren hadn't landed anything since Jack had leaned

up against the door frame and started watching. And Ren was in the Top 1% of the best of the best in the world. Jack had never seen anyone hold their own with him for any amount of time. Only Kali.

They never talked about her newfound and still-escalating skills. Everyone seemed content to watch—like Jack was now—and make notes of tactical capabilities.

Which were many.

Without her coat—wearing a tank top and yoga pants like she currently was—Kali moved with a fluid speed that made her actions hard to spot. Tracking her with direct line of sight put him a beat behind her pace, making her more of a blur than a recognizable body. After some trial and error, Jack had learned to track her movements using peripheral vision.

With her coat, Kali all but disappeared thanks to the chameleon fibers that camouflaged her into the background like a cloak of invisibility. It had taken Kali less than a month to become an A-list lurker in any apparel, but that coat made it so she didn't even have to try to hide while moving full speed—unless she looked you in the eye. Then she became visible for some reason. But anytime she wasn't locking eyes, she was like a dust devil against a wall when she fought in coat-mode. Jack saw everything she stirred up, without ever actually seeing her.

If Muhammad Ali floated like a butterfly and stung like a bee, then Kali flitted like a hummingbird and struck like a whip.

And this one-woman cyclone was Jack's bodyguard for the foreseeable future.

By choice.

Kali wasn't sworn to the Royals like Jack was. She had no obligation to play by their rules but was choosing to stay after a single conversation with Malachi. Last month, the man had broken her out of her self-imposed VR training as a parlor trick. Once the trick had played out, Malachi and Kali had met privately and Kali had walked out of the discussion

9

on Malachi's terms. No arguments; no debates; she was on board now and swore she would stay by Jack's side until she saved his life.

Jack didn't know what the Second Son was playing at by talking Kali into being a Shade. Just like he didn't know if Malachi was behind the scenes now—planting the seeds that would force Kali back onto her old stomping grounds for a high-stakes chase to catch a Starbreaker.

All Jack knew was that he definitely needed Kali on this one, and it was time to see if she was up for joining him.

Pressing a button on his watch, he turned his comm on. "Kali, let's have a chat at your next breaking point."

"Sure, boss," he heard her say, voice even with no strain even as he watched her barrel roll over Ren's swinging leg.

Two seconds later, all motion had stopped on the mat and Ren and Kali tapped fists and stepped apart—Ren's breath was visibly labored; Kali's was not.

She spotted Jack immediately and nodded her head to indicate he should meet her by her locker.

Jack headed over, standing a few feet away as she pulled off her MMA-style gloves. "You're fighting better every time I see you."

"Glad to hear it," she said, starting to undo the wraps while keeping her focus on him. "What's up?"

"A rare opportunity just popped on the radar," he replied, making note of how visible her muscles were with each motion. He knew Ace designed her diet, so she had to be healthy, but there didn't seem to be an ounce of fat on her and her muscle definition looked like it belonged on a man.

Jack was so used to seeing her with her coat on that sometimes he forgot how much power she was packing in her tiny frame.

She sent him a curious look. "An opportunity or a job?"

"An opportunity to face-off against someone big," he replied. "But a big part of it depends on you."

Kali shrugged. "I go where you go."

"That's the thing," Jack replied. "You'd be going alone, and you'd be there to save someone else, not me. I'd stay here and call shots remotely."

He'd have to. Kali was invisible, while Jack could only blend. Ceravene would spot him in a flash. Not being on the playing board was the only advantage Jack had. He had to use it.

Kali's head tilted as if hearing a new sound. "Separating? That's new."

"Yes. But that's not the main concern," Jack confessed.

She finished unwrapping one hand and started on the other. "What's the main concern then?"

"The job is in Los Angeles."

She didn't even pause at the news. She just kept unwrapping and said, "Okay."

Jack felt his eyebrows shoot up in surprise at the fluid response. "Okay?"

Kali gave him an assessing look, taking in his trepidation. "Sure. Why wouldn't it be?"

"Just..." How to phrase it? "All things considered, I thought you might have some concerns about the location."

Kali actually smiled in response. "Do you have any idea how many times simulations have popped me back into that city? How many times it made sure I died there?"

And he was supposed to find that reassuring? Didn't that make things worse?

When he hesitated a beat too long in responding, Kali added, "So long as streets and doors don't start disappearing and turning into contrived kill boxes, I'll be fine. I know that city like the back of my hand and every return trip turns out to be a new adventure." She flashed him a perky thumbs up. "I'm game."

Man. More than once, Jack wondered if he'd done her any favors by sending her to the island and enabling her to spend so much time plugged into the VR world.

But what was done was done.

11

At this point, Jack had to accept that whatever had happened there had transformed Kali into an exception to many rules. So while his experience told him it was too soon to return Kali back where reminders of the life she'd been forced to leave behind would be everywhere she looked, he had to trust the fluid body language in her response.

There was no hitch in her breath, her hands and her eyes stayed steady, and there was genuine mirth in her smirk. Visually speaking, no part of her was stressed at the mention of L.A..

Maybe she was ready.

"What's the gig?" she asked.

"Right now? The gig is to get enough information from a Cupid to stop an assassination scheduled to take place before the new moon."

Kali's eyebrows popped up. "A Cupid? That's a thing?"

Jack nodded. "That's a thing. She'll be back in a few minutes."

"Oh, I'm definitely interested now," she said, both hands free of wraps. "We've never worked with a Cupid before."

"And you won't be," Jack corrected. "She has a related bet on the outcome, so she'll be far away while everything plays out. It would be just you and me. But she may have information that could help us. Want to join the meeting?"

Her nod was immediate. "Definitely. I'm in."

"Good," Jack said, feeling an unexpected rush of relief that did not go unnoticed by Kali.

"You're invested in this case," she observed. "Why?"

Jack hesitated, knowing he had to choose his words carefully. "If we play things right, we may catch a Starbreaker."

"A Starbreaker," Kali echoed, zero comprehension in her voice. "Is that a thing like a Cupid is a thing?"

Again, Jack was very careful as he nodded. "It is."

"I see. And that's all you can say about that?" she deduced.

"That's all I can say about that," he agreed.

It was common practice among all the "suited" to make first impressions through first-person experiences and not through hearsay. Limiting gossip allowed everyone to see what they saw, hear what they heard, and know what they knew when it came to all the other players on the field. In many instances, it cleared the field of tall tales and rumors that served no one but the person spreading them.

The resulting secrecy of this practice seemed to amuse Kali, but this would technically be her first real chance to meet a type she might have some preconceived notions about. Whatever thoughts Kali had about Cupids would be turned on their heads after a few minutes with Wanda.

Maybe then Kali would see why tall tales and hearsay did more harm than good.

And maybe it was time for Jack to let Kali start making her own first impressions by letting her flex a little. She was certainly strong enough in her own right, and he had no doubt Wanda would consider it a pleasure to give Kali her first real taste of the Big Kids' Club.

"Feel like testing your skills a bit?" Jack asked.

"Always," Kali replied, stuffing her hand wraps into a netted bag and tossing the bag over to the hamper. It swished in, of course. Kali didn't miss many shots these days.

"Do your disappearing thing in the meeting," Jack suggested, still not sure what to call it.

Lurking was hanging out in negative space, where eyes rarely focused. It made a person nominally invisible so long as they didn't pull focus through motion.

Blinking involved transporting between spaces. That was about all Jack knew about that, but he did know that when a person blinked, they were gone.

What Kali had been doing these past few weeks was something different altogether and Jack wanted Wanda's read on it.

"Let's see how long you can go without her noticing

you," he said. "I want to see if her skill set can spot you."

Kali grinned as she pulled a towel out of her locker. "I'm game. Usual signal?"

"Usual signal," he said, pulling his lucky coin out of his pocket and giving it a flip. If he ever wanted to know if Kali was in a room, all he had to do was lay the coin face-up. If the coin changed to tails, Kali was close and had his back.

"Cool," Kali said, slinging the towel over her shoulder. "Let me clean up so at least she can't smell me."

Jack didn't mention that she wasn't even sweating.

"Wanda will be back in twenty," he said instead. "See you in Margot's office in fifteen."

"Roger that."

Jack couldn't help but smile at how unconcerned Kali looked at the idea of foiling a Cupid.

She had no idea what she was in for.

Jack may not find Cupid skills particularly useful in his line of work, but that didn't mean they couldn't cold read better than anyone.

"Good luck," he said, starting away.

"If I need luck, I'm doing something wrong."

"Indeed," Jack agreed as they went their separate ways.

Chapter 3

Fourteen minutes later, the elevator doors opened into Margot's office. Ten seconds after that, Jack's coin turned tail-up.

Kali had arrived.

She didn't like to speak when she was doing her invisible thing. She said that the sound waves didn't clear fast enough for her liking and left echoes that resonated long after they were heard … like flavors that lingered after swallowing a bite of food.

Jack knew Wanda was sensitive, but he'd seen nothing to indicate she was *that* sensitive. From his outside perspective, her skills seemed very real-time and people-focused. If he had to guess, he'd say she could read heat signatures, which suggested she would see Kali—invisible or not.

Jack hadn't mentioned as much to Kali, but she wasn't the only one benefitting from this little skills test. Jack might be learning a thing or two as well.

He picked up the coin and gave it a flip before nodding Margot's way. "We're all here."

"Consider this your meeting," Margot replied. "I'll monitor, record, and run the board. After that, I'm out."

"Got it."

Right then, Margot's assistant entered with four glasses of iced tea. Apparently, Wanda hadn't been kidding about that.

"Thank you, Alice," Margot said. "We're ready for Mrs. Amar."

Alice nodded and started out. "I'll send her right in, ma'am."

Margot looked back to Jack. "I've pulled up the profiles of her two soulmates."

Jack nodded.

A beat later, the office door opened and Wanda strutted in like a saleswoman ready to close. She quickly spotted Jack and Margot before giving the rest of the room a cursory glance. Then she did one of her signature long blinks as she read the room in her unique way. Jack had no idea what she saw when she did that, only that she was looking him dead in the eye when her eyes opened again.

Her lips puckered into a dramatic pout. "Jack, I'm disappointed. I was hoping for some Shade with our tea."

Jack paused in honest surprise. Was Wanda playing along, or could she really not sense Kali?

Best to play along either way.

"Everyone is here who needs to be," Jack replied, gesturing to the same seat Wanda had been sitting in before. "Margot has gathered the files for us to reference as we discuss."

"Well, there's not going to be too much paperwork on my Seba," Wanda said, taking her seat. She immediately reached for the tea, stirring the cubes with the straw and taking a small sip. "A few doctors visits while his mom was alive, CPS files documenting their inability to hold on to him, and then dark web transactions since he moved to Los Angeles. Everything he did in New York was analog and off books."

Jack took the seat across from her. "You seem to know a lot about his paper trail. Any reason?"

"Oh, I just checked in on him from time to time. That's

all," she said before taking a sip.

A Cupid *just* checking in from time to time? That was about the same as an obsessed stalker saying they *just* swung by.

"When did you first become aware of Seba?" he asked.

Wanda laughed. "Oh, in another life. Back when I was a law student certain I was going to be the first Black female Supreme Court Justice." She sighed, waxing nostalgic. "Seba was twelve back then and hadn't hit his growth spurt yet. He was just this little white boy selling stuff he'd made or fixed up from a flattened cardboard box I'm pretty sure he slept on at night. He had a regular spot right next to my subway stop."

"Was this after his mom died?" Jack asked, trying to imagine how he could have avoided authorities with a setup like that.

Wanda nodded. "Yeah. She was killed right before his twelfth birthday—which was doubly messed up because she was working extra to afford a nice present for him. Seba was into baseball at the time. She was going to get him a mitt and sign him up for Little League. When she got an unsavory offer and refused, she was murdered in an alley for it. The only thing that kid got for his birthday was a ride to her funeral."

From her desk, Margot cut in. "There are no details about the birthday present in what we have compiled on her. Where did you get that information?"

Wanda shrugged. "Oh, I just asked around with some of her old coworkers."

Jack didn't doubt it. Cupids were notoriously thorough when it came to choosing their marks, and Wanda seemed to have had her eye on this guy for nearly fifteen years. That was a big deal, and meant Wanda was a literal vault of information who could probably talk and tell stories all week.

But they didn't have that kind of time. The new moon was one week away.

Already rolling his lucky coin across his knuckles in

thought, Jack looked Margot's way. "Can you show me pictures of Seba and Vic?"

They were up before he finished asking the question and Jack turned to take a look at the couple for the first time.

Two things were certain at first glance: they weren't ugly and they weren't poor.

"That's my street baby," Wanda cooed, taking another sip. "He gets his fashion sense from his real mama. She was the one who taught him how important it is to dress right for a venue."

"What about his father?" Jack asked.

She rolled her eyes with obvious disgust. "His daddy was a rich boy who went to a Broadway show and saw something on the stage he wanted. He wined and he dined and promised Seba's mama the world. But when his own daddy threatened to cut him off." She made a snipping motion with her fingers. "He cut out. Permanently. Never looked back and never even tried. Seba's mom stayed in her show for as long as her body held its shape. Then she had to choose different work and, ultimately, other stages to dance on."

Jack felt himself tense with disgust at Wanda's summary.

On Jack's list of inexcusable acts, abandoning a child was near the top—especially when one had the means to provide support.

"Seba's father is rich?" Jack asked, just to be sure.

Wanda nodded, clearly not a fan of the man. "Old money. He has a wife and three other kids now. And those kids have done the whole 23andMe thing, so Seba is one DNA test away from having his biological father's full attention." Then she took what could only be described as an overly innocent sip of tea before adding. "Just saying."

Her unspoken implications were as clear as unspoken could be. If Jack needed to play some hardball, there was some ripe fruit for the picking. If, at the end, Seba came into a windfall or some kind of inheritance, Wanda would be a happy Cupid.

But Jack looked up at the man on the screen and knew in his gut that if that guy wanted to find his biological father, his father would already be found.

Still rolling his coin back and forth across the back of his fingers, Jack took another look at the couple.

Blond hair and blue eyes on both. Outside of that, they were a picture of opposites. Where Seba was thick and muscled like a bodyguard in a Hollywood movie, Vic was underweight for her frame and had all the markers of someone whose public persona was heavily handled.

"Do we have any pictures of Vic with friends?" Jack asked Margot.

"No," Wanda answered for her. "Everyone in Vic's life is on her *step-father's*" —she made air quotes with one hand— "payroll."

"Step-father?" Jack asked. "Not 'adoptive father' or just 'father'?"

Wanda rolled her eyes, head shaking. "According to the think tank Bauer hired when he adopted her, three syllables—like 'adopted'—draws too much attention to itself. And having Vic refer to Evan as her 'new father' left a bad taste in the mouths of her parents' fans. 'Step-family' may not be technically accurate when it comes to Vic's relationship with the Bauers, but it scored the highest in the think tank so that's what they've rolled with."

Bauer had outsourced what his adopted child should call him? Vic hadn't had a vote in the matter?

That told Jack more than anything else so far.

"Anyway," Wanda continued, "all that is an aside to the fact that, if you find a picture of Vic with friends, she's either with fans or actors paid to play her friends before reporting her activities back to step-daddy."

That was such heavy-handed monitoring, Jack had to wonder if it stopped there. "What's her security situation?"

"She has rotating guards who accompany her any time she leaves the Bauer property."

"And I'm guessing they're on Evan Bauer's payroll, too?"

"Mmhmm," she said, taking another sip. "I see you're getting the picture when it comes to Vic's situation."

"I think I am," he agreed. "But I'm missing how the Bauer family ended up adopting her."

"Then you need to come down from your high tower every so often, honey. Because everyone knows the Vic Davalos adoption story."

Jack leaned back in chair. "What's the shorthand on that saga?"

Wanda perked right up at the question, placing her tea to the side and angling to face him. "Oooh. Where to start on that one?"

"Who were her parents?" Jack asked.

"Raphael and Evelyn Davalos," Wanda replied. "Think Kurt Cobain and Courtney Love, only behind the scenes—a songwriting duo writing hit after hit after hit while sharing a drug problem. Evan Bauer got them writing exclusively for his label and quickly became both their enabler and exploiter. He also upped the ante when it came to their drug of choice and kept them supplied to keep the hits coming. No one had time for rehab so they just cleaned up messes and looked the other way when red flags started popping up like middle-aged acne. Raph and Eve were pulling in a steady cash flow and Bauer didn't want to say bye-bye to that—especially since addicts aren't really all that good at counting their pennies and Bauer was taking them for a ride. Just like he's taking their daughter for a ride now by hiding her inheritance and siphoning money out of her active income to pay for his 'services'."

"Like her friends and security?" Jack guessed.

Wanda grinned. "No one ever called you a stupid man, Jack."

No. They didn't. And Jack didn't like the picture he was starting to see come together.

"Vic's parents overdosed the same night," Wanda added. "It's believed that the father's was accidental. Autopsies show he died about three hours before his wife. And we know Vic's mom called a few people and left panicked voicemails before apparently deciding to join him. But since those calls happened at two in the morning and no one had their ringers on, it was Vic who found them the next morning and called 9-1-1."

Wow. Heartbreaking. Simply heartbreaking. Vic and Seba had traumatic childhoods that managed to be similar and opposite at the same time.

One lost his parents to abandonment and murder before growing up an orphan on the streets; the other lost her parents to overdose and ended up in a guarded mansion.

"How did Vic end up with a producer and not with family members after they passed?"

Wanda rolled her eyes, looking like she had a mental list of people she wanted to smack on that account. "In short? Money. The family didn't really want her and Bauer convinced them he could provide for her better."

"Why would he want to do that?"

"Because he'd been caught embezzling and needed to" — the air quotes came out again— "*create a situation* that changed the headlines in his favor in order to not be forced into stepping down from control of his companies. Basically, he needed good PR so he hitched his wagon to the orphan of the hour to control the narrative."

Disgusting. "And is he the one who hired Ceravene?"

Wanda scowled like she wanted to say yes but ended up shrugging instead. "There is no evidence to that effect, if that's what you're asking."

It was. Jack didn't operate on hunches. He only gave them a door to walk through onto a stage of his making. So Jack would leave a door open for the step-father to reveal himself, but he had to keep his mind open to other outcomes and unforeseen villains.

He looked back up at the two beautiful people on the screen—paying particular attention to their eyes.

Seba had the gaze of a man who took care of business and called no other man his boss. Trust issues and no respect for authority were almost certain. He looked like a man who esteemed exactly one quality in others: competence. Which made sense when overlaid onto a life growing up alone on the streets of New York. The streets did not reward half-measures.

The weak of mind or heart did not survive in such a stark environment.

Jack felt he might have a good sense of what made Seba tick, but his portrait of Vic was much less conclusive. Considering she was the assassin's alleged target, he needed to fix that.

"Margot, can I get a collage of Vic pics?"

A moment later, the woman's Instagram feed appeared on the screen. While the bio described her as a fashion model, Jack saw a whole lot more skin than clothes. But it was her eyes that interested him.

In the staged shots, she had an obvious tigress persona—eyes bold, often sending daring looks into the camera lens in the few shots where her face was the focus. Most of the shots were zoomed in, highlighting her assets, with her face cropped out.

"Now candid shots," Jack prompted.

The pictures that filled the screen next confirmed his suspicions.

Pictures with fans were a repeat of the same practiced expression—no authenticity, all muscle memory. She'd probably spent hours perfecting that pose under strict supervision, yet Jack doubted anyone would believe she was anything but an empowered woman who did whatever she wanted.

For a beat, he wished Claire was sitting next to him so she could provide her insight on the woman. Expressions and microexpressions were her specialties, but since she wouldn't be weighing in for another 141 days, Jack would have to get what he could out of Wanda.

"One question," he said, turning to her.

"Only one?" she teased.

He smiled. "Only one on the topic of soulmates."

That got her full attention and she turned to face him. "Ooh. I'm listening."

"There are five types of soulmates and these two are obviously the wound-mate type. Aren't they supposed to be terrible romantic partners?"

"Well, look at you knowing something about something you claim you don't believe in," she replied, looking pleased.

He shrugged, playing along with her baiting vibe. "Doubt is no excuse for ignorance."

"Mmhmm," she drawled. "I'll make a believer out of you yet. But, to answer your question: yes, they are wound mates. And, yes, wound mates make terrible long-term romantic partners. But the game changes when a person only has one soulmate left on the earth—which is Seba's situation." She wiggled her eyebrows. "If every other soulmate dies, the last one left holds the possibilities of those that are gone. So, if you pay attention, you'll notice that Seba and Vic meet the requirements for all five types of mates. That creates a four-to-one situation that can only end one of two ways."

She said that last part as if she thought Jack would fill in the blanks without help. He couldn't.

"Come now. This is one time you don't need to over think, Jack," Wanda said when he took a beat too long to comprehend what she was getting at. "Think of every romantic tale that withstands the test of time. Think Romeo and Juliet versus Cinderella."

"Ah, they're either 'star-crossed' or 'happily ever after'," he said, seeing what she was getting at this time.

She tapped a finger to her nose like he'd nailed it.

"That's right. Those are the only choices left when you're

down to one last soulmate on earth. And my little Seba has way too much potential to waste on that star-crossed nonsense. I'll tell you that right now." She pointed up to the pictures of Vic on the screen. "The world needs this power couple. But they'll only work as a couple. If Vic dies, Seba will spend the rest of his days a nihilist who only lives for himself. And that's pretty much the opposite of what the world needs."

She punctuated her speech by stirring the cubes in her glass with the straw before draining the glass and setting it to the side.

"What are his skills?" Jack asked, and suddenly Wanda's face was a comical mask of innocence.

"Hmm?"

"You said Seba has too much potential to waste on a star-crossed fate," Jack pressed. "What kind of potential are we talking about?"

All of a sudden, Wanda got a lot more vague. "Oh, you know, whatever Vic inspires him to be."

What was with the sudden shiftiness? "Uh-huh. And if Vic inspired him to be something, what might that something turn out to be?"

He knew it was the right question to ask the moment it came out of his mouth. He couldn't believe he hadn't seen it sooner. Wanda hadn't just been playing matchmaker with Seba all these years.

She'd been playing recruiter.

Just like Wanda had been drawn out of law school and into her potential by her husband, Wanda had her eye on Seba, and probably Vic, for stepping into higher potential. And she knew exactly what that potential was. No question.

"Wanda," he said in a warning tone when she delayed her answer. "You just told me no one accuses me of being a stupid person."

She shrugged. "What can I say? At the moment, they're both just regular people."

24

He phrased his next question carefully. "But are there any skills I should be aware of?"

"Well, he's ... street smart," Wanda said, still skirting.

"Obviously," Jack replied. "What else?"

"He's an excellent fighter," she added.

Coming from the wife of Titus, that was no small claim. "What else?"

She rolled her eyes and groaned. "Okay, I might have dropped some Robin Hood literature in his tip jar a time or two."

Robin Hood literature?

Wanda thought Seba had the potential to be a Robin Hood? That changed everything.

"What kind of literature?" he asked

"Nothing special," Wanda said with a shrug. "Just some pages out of the Book of Hooding is all."

Oh. *Just* the manual.

"Which pages?" Jack pressed.

"Only the main chapter pages," she confessed dismissively.

"The pages that summarize all the content in the following chapter in bullet points?" Jack clarified.

"Sure," she said with a shrug. "That sounds right. I mean, I know it's against the rules for me to give him the actual book. Another Robin Hood has to make the hand off. I know that. And I technically didn't give him the chapter pages. I just put them somewhere he *might* find them."

Might? She'd put them in a place where he would definitely find them. "Did he read them?"

She shrugged, back to being shifty. "How would I know? I never asked."

Jack had to assume he had, and that changed the game entirely. It meant Seba could read types as well as he could fight. It meant he knew how to hit a mark. It meant he had fluency in multiple languages, knew how to use costumes and camouflage, and had an instinct to make the rich and powerful prove their mettle.

Suddenly the glint in the man's eyes that Jack had seen in his pictures made a whole lot more sense.

"What about his band of men?" Jack asked.

"What about 'em?" Wanda asked, once again trying to play dumb. Jack couldn't help but think it was Margot's presence in the room that had the Cupid worried there might be some repercussions for covertly nurturing an orphan into something she had no business playing mentor to.

But Wanda had to decide which was more important to her—saving lives or keeping secrets.

"Does he have a band of men?" he pressed.

"Not that he knows of," Wanda hedged.

"Any that you know of?"

When he heard the resigned sigh, he knew she'd finally caved. "Ugh. Fine. Yes, okay? He's got some fans who could easily be banded if he feels so inclined. Happy?"

The nervous look she sent Margot after that confession confirmed Jack's suspicions but he had no pity as he pushed on. "And where are these men?"

"Online," Wanda confessed. "The dark web. On the site Seba uses for his private contract work. Everything's anonymous but users see each other's screen names, feedback, and message board responses. Users can post questions for others to answer, and Seba has a record of being 100% helpful in his responses. Some of his responses have even saved other users' lives or kept them out of prison."

That didn't sound like a band that would present much of a threat at this point. Such men were probably located all around the world.

"So he's got some goodwill going with a bunch of online peers?"

"Basically," Wanda agreed. "But we're talking former military and well-funded conspiracy theorists in full fanboy mode. Trust me, they're all down to impress him. If he ever sent out a signal that he was putting a team together, the pool of recruits he'd be able to talk out of their bunkers would blow your mind. They know an Alpha when they see one."

To most of the world, the term alpha was generic. But it had a very specific meaning in the Book of Hooding, denoting a person who held space with a near-supernatural awareness of everything that happened within their territory.

"So Seba's an Alpha?" Jack asked, point blank.

"Put it this way," she said, leaning in against the arm of her chair. "When I checked in on him yesterday, he spotted me watching him from thirty yards off while I was looking at him with my eyes closed."

"And you were going to let me go into this situation without knowing that?" Jack objected. "That's kind of key strategic information, Wanda."

That got him another shrug. "It's nothing a Pimpernel can't handle, right?"

No. But it was something that definitely needed to be calculated in advance.

"Well, I have to confess," Kali said, suddenly sitting on the arm of Wanda's chair. "This sounds more interesting by the minute. When do we start?"

There was a freeze of shocked silence from Wanda as she spun around to take in the woman who was suddenly sidled in next to her.

Her eyes grew wide as saucers before she did one of her slow blinks as her hand reached out to make contact with Kali's clothed arm. Then she took in both Margot and Jack's non-reaction to her appearance and spoke.

"Is this the part where you tell me why we're not calling security?"

Jack fought the urge to laugh. In all honesty, he'd forgotten Kali was in the room.

"Wanda, this is my Shade. She'll be working with me on this."

Wanda's jaw literally dropped, her mouth forming an

oval. "This snack-size Bellatrix is your Shade?"

Kali blinked in surprise at that description but bounced back quickly when Wanda added, "A *girl*?"

Kali's eyes narrowed. "You got a problem with that?"

"Me?" Wanda laughed. "Heavens, no! I'm all for a woman who doesn't invoke the rights of the damsel card when she's saved and actually pays her debts. But I have to tell you that, while your blinking ability is seriously impressive, my Seba will notice blinking on his turf like a strobe light in a bedroom. You'll get maybe three pops in before you become the top concern on his radar. So you can't be leaning on that skill in this case. It'll only pull focus."

"I don't know how to blink," Kali confessed.

That got a new pause out of Wanda. Then a, "Whaaaat?"

"It's true," Jack replied for her, hiding a smile of his own. "She's been in this room the entire time. I wanted to see if she could trick you, then forgot she was here once we got started. It's something that happens more often than I would like."

Next to him, Wanda looked shellshocked. "You've been here?"

Kali nodded.

"In this room?"

Another nod.

"Since I walked in?" Wanda pressed.

"Yes," Kali confirmed. "Why did you call me a Bellatrix?"

Wanda's tension faded as she laughed. "Honey, have you looked in a mirror? If not, I'm pretty sure every person you've ever met has mentioned that you've got some pretty signature eyes there. And I've been around the globe enough to know which tribe married into *that* DNA strand for eye color."

Just like that, Kali looked like the one off-balance and Jack felt content to sit back and see how things would shake out between the two women.

28

While Kali faltered—for once—Wanda pounced. "You got a name, tiny?"

"Kali," she replied, sounding a little uncertain. That wasn't good.

"Uh-huh," Wanda drawled, clearly seeing right through her. "You got a last name, Kali?"

"Fischer," Kali replied, a bit faster this time. "Kali Fischer."

"Mmhmm," Wanda said, looking her up and down as she pulled out her phone and opened an app. "And how long has that been your name, Ms. Kali Fischer?"

Kali recovered quickly. "Ever since I entered this crazy world."

Misleading, but technically accurate.

"Right," Wanda drawled, not sounding impressed as she scrolled down her screen and eventually clicked on something. "Did you receive a personality profile with your new name and birth chart, Kali?"

Kali's cool reserve returned in full. "I don't believe in profiles and horoscopes."

"I can see that," Wanda said, eyes finished with what was on her screen and now looking at Kali like a cat that had a mouse cornered. "And I thank you for it. Because it allows me to see you quite clearly, indeed, Ms. Definitely-Not Kali Fischer and Definitely-Not a Sagittarius" She looked her up and down. "I peg you as a Leo."

Kali didn't back down. "Is that so?"

Wanda smiled. "That is so. The bad news is that someone needs to talk some sense into you if you plan on doing anything but hiding in the shadows for the rest of your life. The good news is that you're good enough for now. Your lurking skills are almost certainly solid enough to keep my Seba and his soulmate safe while staying off his radar. Just don't ever look him in the eye. He'll tag you in a beat."

"I'll remember that," Kali said.

"Please do," Wanda said with authority. "Eyes are the

windows to the soul, and Hearts rule the soul. I'll warn you now, since it could mean the difference between succeeding and failing, that once my boy Seba gets a peek into your soul you won't be able to hide so easily from him anymore."

Kali's head tilted as if she doubted as much.

"He is no novice," Wanda added, not missing the look. "Untrained? Sure. But he still has impeccable instincts. And while you may be quite good at blending into air, if he gets a connection with you—like I'm getting with you right now— he'll start noticing you like something burning on the stove. He won't even have to see you. He'll just sense you like something in the air."

Well, that was a bit of a change of tune from a few minutes ago.

Last Jack had heard, Wanda had been hedging at Seba *maybe* having a few skills. Now, all of a sudden, he was a bloodhound with a sixth sense?

The subtext was clear: Jack had to assume he was dealing with a Robin Hood in all things related to Sebastian Kahn.

Appearing intrigued at the prospect, Kali took Wanda's bait. "How will he do that?"

"By sensing what you hide," Wanda said gently, as if she knew exactly what those things were. "It will become a signature he picks up, sight unseen—like smelling bread and knowing on instinct if it's baked just right or it's burning. Because, in the end, there are only two flavors of heat between people: love and fear."

Kali's head tilted as if that intrigued her, but she stayed silent.

Wanda tapped a finger to her temple. "If you come at this job with your head, the only flavor on the table is what you fear. So, if you're not careful, that's what Seba will get a whiff of: your worst fears, lurking. Smelling yours will make him consider his, and I think you can see how that is a recipe for doing things the hard way."

In Jack's experience, people ultimately trusted their eyes

when given something convincing to look at, but Kali rode blind spots. Wanda made a good point that people might start trusting phantom instincts in that situation—Hearts, in particular.

Staying off the radar of Ceravene might not be Kali's only challenge in what was about to come.

"So how do I avoid that?" Kali asked.

Wanda flashed her signature smile. "Let go of your secrets, baby girl," she said, her hand gesturing like she was letting go of a balloon. "Secrets are highly charged fears and, the more charged something is, the brighter it burns. And heat knows heat, which means the very first thing any true Heart knows of you is the love you hold and fears you hide. They glow for us—calling like a lighthouse to your harbor. And once we tangle with your heat, we're in. So you must be very careful about how you choose to hide a thing."

Jack leaned back in his seat, happy to have Wanda educate Kali on such matters.

Jack might have a bit of a reputation for being dismissive as to what Hearts brought to the table, but that was because Hearts chased chaos where Diamonds sought perfection.

Tactically speaking, they were cats and dogs when it came to field work.

As Wanda had pointed out, Hearts followed the heat in any moment. The quality made them fickle and terrible at following plans. They could follow a path to a point—like a flame following a gasoline trail—but were just as likely to spread flames of chaos with anything else that caught their attention along the path.

There were few things a magician needed less than an impulsive and fickle assistant with a heartfelt passion for chasing squirrels.

Margot, of course, was the exception to the rule. The woman was so zoomed out on her readings that her bursts of heat were often perceived as ice by the receiver. Margot was special in many regards, but her ability to hold a course and manage her impulsivity definitely made her stand out among her kind.

As Royalty, she was forbidden from mentoring anyone unassigned to her, but Wanda had no such restrictions. So Jack pressed his lips together in silence and let Kali learn from a master.

"My Seba might be a little lost right now," Wanda continued. "But it's likely that being around Vic will wake up his heart. He might start to see. So let him see what he sees, and let him think of it what he will. To hide, you cannot glow with what you'd wish him not to know. You must be free as a breeze with no thought of itself. Release all fears of being seen, even if he spots you, and Seba will focus elsewhere. Understood?"

Kali's nod came slowly. "Yeah. I think so."

Every time Jack had been around Wanda, she'd been flighty and coy. Her claim that she had once wanted to be a lawyer and a judge had never really rung true until that moment. Maybe he needed to rethink working with another Heart after Margot retired—although he was mostly still in denial Margot's retirement was ever going to happen at all.

"Good!" Wanda said, her smile and bubbly mood returning in a flash as she looked Kali up and down. "Now, tell me what in the world you are, girl. Because I have four guesses, and no one likes a curious Cupid. How about you put me out of my misery? What's your calling card?"

Kali's confusion was genuine. "What do you mean?"

Wanda rolled her eyes. "C'mon, honey. Keep up. I'm a Cupid; he's a Pimpernel; and our host is a little under a year away from being a Queen. So what does that make you?"

Kali shrugged. "I don't know. I popped out of a box last month and this is my life now. I don't think I have a title outside of Shade."

Wanda blinked three times—slowly—then turned to Jack for further explanation. "Popped out of a box? Translation, please?"

Jack didn't miss Margot's cautionary look, reminding him of the details he was not allowed to reference—mainly everything referencing the Royals and the Day of Anemone. He had to tread carefully.

"Kali spent a few years in VR simulations," Jack replied. "And, since waking up here, she has yet to be fully convinced she's not still in one."

"A few years?" Wanda gawked. "Girl, didn't anyone tell you to consult a doctor in cases of simulations lasting longer than six hours?"

That got a laugh out of Kali. "I'll remember that next time."

Smiling to herself, Wanda looked Kali up and down. Then the smile changed to concern. "You're going to go out there and help my Seba thinking all this is a simulation?"

Kali shrugged. "Does it make a difference?"

Wanda nodded. "Yes. Yes, it does." She tapped a finger over her heart. "Here. So tell me what's got you thinking this is a simulation?"

Kali didn't even blink. "Tell me who the President of the United States is."

There was a beat of frozen silence. Then Wanda threw her head back and laughed long enough and hard enough to have to wipe a tear from her eye before looking at Jack.

"She's got a point." Then she started toward the door and turned her focus back to Kali. "Try not to screw this up. I'd love to work with you again."

"We'll do what we can," Kali replied as Jack stood from his seat.

"Are we done?" he asked.

Wanda stopped by the door and nodded. "I just got the warmest little feeling in my stomach that I'm going to win my bet. It's time to let you two do whatever it is you do while I get out of your business."

It felt abrupt, but Jack wasn't arguing. He felt like he had what he needed, too.

From the door, Wanda gave him an almost maternal look. "You, my friend, have a unique ability to surround yourself with amazing women. I haven't been giving you enough credit."

"Uh, thanks?" he replied.

"You're welcome." She looked at Kali next. "And you … no one is born a Shade, my dear. So if you don't think this world is real but you want to know who you are in it, listen to how people describe you when you're not around, and maybe you'll figure out who you are before I do."

Kali nodded. "I'll do that."

Jack crossed the room to Wanda and held out his hand for a farewell shake. "We'll do our best for Seba and Vic."

"I believe that," Wanda said with a smile as their hands clasped together. "I'll still be stalking you from a distance, but don't take that personally. It's just me driving myself crazy by caring too much."

"Just don't pull focus and we should be fine," Jack replied, releasing her hand.

"Me? Not pull focus?" she teased.

Jack laughed. "Do it for Seba."

"For Seba," Wanda agreed before looking up to where Margot still sat. "Thank you for your grace in this matter. I'll never forget it."

The only response Margot made was a tip of her head, which Wanda returned, before showing herself out.

When she was gone, Kali looked his way. "Well, that was interesting. What's next?"

"I want you on the ground in L.A. as soon as possible to scout out the situation," he decided. "Gather everything you think you need and visit me in the scenario room when you're ready to leave."

Kali sent him a quick salute. "Roger that, boss."

34

Chapter 4

Standing in the large cube of his scenario room, Jack took in the sea of holographic people scheduled to interact with Vic Davalos over the next week. It was too much to process at once. He needed to simplify.

"Ace," he instructed the AI, "let's keep Vic and Seba on the board and remove everyone else but the Bauers and any personnel with one-on-one access to Vic."

In a flash, 127 players became nine.

Much better.

Jack felt like he could breathe again even if he had no idea where to start. Every tactic he knew had to be in a Starbreaker's handbook. He had to bring something new to the table, which would be doubly challenging since he was going into the game at a disadvantage. He wouldn't have Claire's near-endless observations to filter his ideas through in the planning stage. Margot was out, too, due to Royal conflicts of interest.

Jack needed to figure this out by himself and, while he was accustomed to starting cases with more to go on than rumors from a Cupid, he'd also started with less. At least Wanda had handed him firm targets and a timeline.

A *short* timeline, yes, but workable.

He needed to choose how he wanted to approach his possibly one-and-only attempt at snaring one of the most heartless villains known to man. It was one thing to murder; it was another thing altogether to frame someone into appearing like a person they never were before wiping them from the earth.

That's what Starbreakers did.

People often spoke of changing their stars as a metaphor for changing the circumstances they were born into. A Starbreaker flipped a person's stars upside-down and took a picture for posterity before sending their target crashing to the earth like a flaming meteor forever remembered by its scars and scourges.

If Wanda's accusations checked out, and Ceravene really was after Vic Davalos, that said a lot about the Instagram model. It meant someone wanted Vic's potential off the planet and that a Starbreaker had taken an objective look at the woman and accepted the challenge.

Jack needed to find a way to keep Vic's stars as they were: unbroken.

"Let's take a look at her schedule," he said to the AI. "Display a linear timeline of locations in Vic Davalos's itinerary over the next week."

As quickly as Jack spoke, Ace projected the locations on the far wall like images on an old film roll. Ace also included summaries of the negotiated terms for each of the 32 negotiated appearances.

About an average of five locations per day. Some modeling shoots; multiple paid party appearances; one full day of filming; several meetings with sponsors; and three TV interviews.

Vic Davalos might have a professional reputation of being an irresponsible party girl, but a schedule like hers would demand discipline and punctuality to pull off. It was unlikely the real woman was anything like the persona she portrayed in the media. But if someone wanted to kill her with minimum suspicion, they would likely play into her public reputation. It would be the path of least suspicion for someone wanting to get away with murder.

"Grey-out private meetings and corporate locations," Jack instructed, and 17 of the slides faded, leaving 15 in full color. Mostly photo shoots, club visits, brand ambassador visits, and house parties.

"Grey-out photo shoots," he said and watched three more panels dim, leaving him with 9 key players and 12 possible crime scenes.

Much more manageable.

When it came to implementing technology into his work process, Jack had always been a late-adapter. He was old-school at heart, preferring analog over digital 99 times out of 100. But even he had to admit that traditional war boards didn't hold a candle to standing in a holographic scenario room. Jack could study all the players and environments before taking them on dry runs with an AI tossing out red flags on faulty assumptions.

It led to much fewer errors in a real-world environment.

The first time Jack misjudged the known aptitudes of a player, Ace made their avatar glow red. The second time Jack miscalculated, the scenario froze and Ace filled Jack in on where he'd gone wrong. On jobs that required it, he could also practice impersonations he needed to pull off while the AI graded him on things like posture, gait, and cadence.

So, while Jack still liked to keep with tradition when it came to everything else, his war board was permanently retired in storage. The scenario room was vastly superior.

But Jack wasn't at the scenario phase in this case. He was still getting to know the couple Wanda was so passionate about.

For example, it turned out Wanda's street baby was a conman.

Wanda had conveniently left out that fact.

Seba wasn't a full grifter, though. He made his living as a

fixer and ringer for people willing to pay his hefty fee. Based on his work history, Seba was mostly hired to test loyalties in personal or business relationships.

When a high-roller worried something wasn't as it seemed, Seba was the guy who showed up pretending to be someone he wasn't and lured targets into revealing their true colors. Then he reported back and let his employers use the information how they saw fit.

On the surface, Seba ran a business that was barely more than a bare-bones web page. But on the dark web, he was quite well-known as *Archer310* and had a customer satisfaction record of 99.8%.

Ironically, Archer310's one negative write-up came from Evan Bauer himself. Apparently, Seba had charmed the wrong target and been immediately removed from the only job Bauer had ever offered him.

There was definitely a story there.

Outside of Evan Bauer's scathing review, Archer310 had a track record of repeat customers who vouched for an impressive array of skills. Everything from social fluidity to gameplay to physical prowess.

Growing up on the streets may have been hard on Seba, but it had shaped him into a very formidable man who had received over $6 million in wire transfers or Bitcoin since moving to Los Angeles.

Jack looked at the holographic representation of Seba standing across from him. Six-foot-four with the muscles of a man who pushed himself on a daily basis.

"All those skills?" Jack muttered. "Just to dupe people?"

It was a shame, really. Not only was it a waste of talent, but it seemed the lifestyle had driven Seba into a life of near-total social isolation in his off hours. He'd built no social circle since moving to L.A.. His only known associates were professionals like him.

Seba Kahn didn't form attachments. He worked angles, got paid, and moved on like clockwork. It was an isolating pattern with no positive trajectory. If Seba wasn't already in a downward spiral, he would be soon.

In contrast, Jack found Vic's social circle far too crowded to be genuine, with all her closest relationships on her payroll.

Jack didn't know which was worse, voluntarily having no friends or having friends who were influenced by paychecks.

Regardless, Jack was starting to see what Wanda was talking about when she said she saw Vic and Seba as every type of soulmate wrapped into one. Because, yes, they were wound mates, but they were also mirrors—also known as "reflected inverses"—Seba being anti-social, Vic being overly social ... Seba having a reputation of hyper-competence while Vic was famous for being a dumb party girl.

In many ways, Vic and Seba were two sides of a coin. And while Jack didn't necessarily believe that made two people soulmates, he did know opposites noticed each other in a room, as did people who shared core pain points.

If people like Wanda wanted to call that dynamic "soulmates" and claim there were five kinds, that was fine with Jack, but it didn't help him with his job.

Jack had to build plans on what was certain. He needed an infrastructure that could be counted on at 100%, not 20%. Things like the fact that Vic's step-mom and step-sister were scheduled to leave for Paris in 48 hours and Vic's step-father would be leaving for Tokyo three days after that.

All the Bauers would be out-of-town starting two days before the new moon and one day after it started waxing again.

Vic was the only one staying in Los Angeles.

It wasn't proof there was a plot against her but, if there was, her family would all conveniently have solid alibis.

Jack stepped away from Seba and walked over to Vic's hologram, which stood a few inches taller than Jack. Next to her, in a line, stood the only five personnel Vic was ever completely alone with: four bodyguards—Ryan, Tristan, Chloe, and Bret—and her manager, Nora.

Chloe worked nights, sleeping in Vic's private wing of the Bauer mansion ... something that struck Jack as odd.

Why would Vic need personal security in one of the most secure homes in the city? Among his many holdings, Evan Bauer owned a home security business. If there was a bell or whistle, he had it. Yet Vic clearly didn't trust it ... or someone didn't trust her.

There were no clear records revealing which was the case.

What Jack did know was that, come 6:00 a.m., Chloe clocked out and Ryan, Tristan, or Bret clocked in. One of them shadowed her in plain clothes when she visited secure locations, and two flanked her in dark suits when she went out in public.

Outside of Vic's home, guards stayed close, with the exception of Nora's office. Those meetings were private and neither woman kept digital notes, which meant even Ace didn't know what was discussed outside of Vic's resulting schedule and press releases.

There might be a fifteen year age gap between the two women, but it was clear that Nora was more than a manager to Vic. Based on retrieved texts, Nora did her best to advocate for Vic but often still came out on the losing end of exchanges with the Bauers.

Ryan, Tristan, Chloe, Bret, and Nora.

If there were five people in the world Vic trusted with her life and reputation, Jack was looking at them. Anyone who wanted to kill Vic would have to bypass one of those five by either corrupting or outplaying them.

The question was: How and where would they fail her?

Jack was busy compiling possible options when the main door opened and Kali walked in carrying a couple of books. She looked around, seeming to take in his lack of progress at a glance before holding up a book in each hand for him to see.

Ah, so she finally found it.

"I'm guessing you knew Margot has a rather massive library in a climate-controlled sub-level of this building," she said.

"I did."

Kali tsked her tongue. "All that wisdom on a shelf and you never told me?"

Jack grinned. "You never asked."

"Right," she drawled. "The whole 'you gotta ask to receive' thing even applies to finding libraries?"

"Especially to libraries," Jack said. "What books did you request?"

She wiggled the book in her right hand first. "That Book of Hooding you two were talking about in the meeting." She wiggled the other book. "And this one on the five types of soulmates Wanda kept referencing. I was expecting something new and enlightening, but it's just a collection of famous stories categorized into variations of soulmate pairings."

"Yep," Jack said. "Sounds like you're all caught up on soulmate theory."

His sarcasm pulled a smile out of her, but she didn't comment on it.

"Did Wanda happen to mention to you which type of pairing she thinks Seba and Vic are?" she asked instead.

"She didn't," Jack said, knowing they could still ask if Kali felt strongly about it. Not that it would do them any good.

"Bummer," Kali said. "I was going to lay a wager on this being a Rapunzel situation where he saves her from the tower and she saves him from being lost."

"Well, between us, I'm pretty sure Wanda has no idea which fairy tale they are," Jack said, trying to keep his tone neutral. "Cupids are notorious for only matching couples to archetypes after the fact. They just fly by the seat of their pants while following whatever silver linings they can drum up in the chaos. And when everything shakes out, they claim it was all meant to be and tie it to a fairy tale."

Jack didn't realize how much he'd overshared until he saw Kali was pressing her lips together not to interrupt him. She looked amused.

"Not a fan of Cupids, huh?"

Caught red-handed. "Sorry. I should have kept those thoughts to myself."

"It's fine," Kali replied, still looking amused. "I can handle it."

Jack shook his head. "For the record, this is exactly why Royals require their pledges to train through first-hand experience and mentorships." Like Claire was doing that very moment. "Learning through hearsay always introduces bias. It's best to learn from actual practitioners, not skeptics."

"I get that," Kali agreed. "But understanding your bias is equally as important to helping you as understanding Wanda's take."

"Maybe," he said, sending a pointed glance at the books in her hand. "But there is a lot to be said for the bias introduced during a first exposure to something—including learning from a book. Reading and hearsay can convey knowledge and concepts, but wisdom comes by way of experience. Words without experience can be easily twisted into fallacies forever misattributed as truth."

Kali's eyebrows popped up. "Is that an official Royal doctrine or a Jack Original?"

He let out a short laugh. "A little bit of both. Anyway, the point is, it's best to learn from a mentor and be reminded by texts. Learning from books results in unpredictable levels of comprehension. So I'm saying that, while I'm glad you're going to read those books before heading out on this job, I don't want you to get in the habit of reading to learn. If you want to understand something, seek a mentor first so you have a sense of the mindset the texts are being applied to.

You'll be glad you did."

"Good advice," Kali agreed with a nod. "Maybe then I'll start to understand why every type seems to disagree on how many types of people there are. The Royals say there are 53 profiles with 14 tiers and four types" —she held up the books, wiggling them in turn— "Cupids say it all boils down to five types of pairings, while the Book of Hooding claim there are six individual roles in society. No one seems to agree."

"Because different types have different jobs," Jack replied, gesturing to the holograms. "Anytime someone goes to work, they need a system for prioritizing workflow. To someone like Wanda, only lovers matter." He pointed to Vic and Seba. "With everything in this case, she only cares what happens with Vic and Seba. Starting a dumpster fire in anyone else's life is an acceptable tactic if it keeps those two holding hands. Then she'll claim all the interference she created to force them together is some undeniable cosmic gravity that pulled them together naturally."

Kali looked over at the holograms. "Well, Vic and Seba are both hot. I don't think natural attraction is off the table."

Jack ignored her snark and continued answering her question by pointing only at Seba. "Conversely, a Robin Hood keeps eyes on everyone, always watching for unmet needs and looming threats. He has to or he'll be taken out by a nemesis or even a stalker sooner than not. To avoid that, he or she only needs to see the world in six types."

"Huh," Kali said thoughtfully. "Such a practical answer. I wasn't expecting that. Everything else in your world is so weird."

His world? Like she wasn't standing right next to him in it? "I'm the weird one here? I beg to differ."

"Touché," Kali laughed before eyeing the row of nine main players and seeming to sort them in her own mind before asking, "So how many types of people are there in the Pimpernel world?"

"Two," Jack replied. "Those who cooperate, and those who don't."

She seemed to find that amusing. "How do you know who will cooperate in advance?"

"You don't," he replied, his eyes returning to the line up before directing his voice toward the ceiling. "Ace, put everyone back on the stage."

The next moment, 127 holograms stood in the space. A sea of blank faces staring back at them.

"What I need to do is create a scenario that allows everyone you see now to self-sort as they go," he explained. "If we set the stage right, cooperation looks like anyone acting within their usual status quo. And all we have to do is let them." He rapped his knuckle against the Book of Hooding in her hand. "In Robin Hood terms, anyone who cooperates is like a Gamma. Those who—"

"—turn the tide by turning with the tide," Kali finished, quoting the definition verbatim.

"Right," Jack said, surprised she'd both read the information already and retained it. "A non-cooperator is anyone who doesn't turn with that tide and keeps trying to push things toward a self-serving endgame. A Robin Hood would call that type a Sigma."

"Those who feed off their own to grow," Kali added, again quoting the text exactly.

"Yes," he agreed. "A Sigma's endgame demands they change something in the status quo to meet their goals. They are allergic to cooperation and are always influencing others to clear the path for them."

She arched a skeptical brow. "It's L.A.. We're going to see a lot of that kind of behavior."

"And we'll vet it as we go, letting go of everything that doesn't lead back to Ceravene."

She still looked unconvinced. "But if a Starbreaker behaved like a standard Sigma, wouldn't someone have spotted and caught one long ago?"

"It's hard to know." Was she onto something there?

Kali stacked the *Tales of Soulmates* book on top of *The Book of Hooding* and started leafing through it. "If a Starbreaker was a character in a soulmate story, who would they be?"

He'd never been asked that before so it took a moment to find a fitting answer.

"Think of the story of Snow White, and imagine the Huntsman was heartless," he decided. "That would match up with a Starbreaker."

She found the story in the book with surprising speed and asked, "How so?"

"Well, you have the evil queen looking in a mirror asking, '*Mirror, Mirror, on the wall, who's the fairest of them all?*' And when she gets the answer that she's Fairest #2, what does she do?"

"Enlists the Huntsman to bring her Snow White's heart," Kali replied.

"Right," Jack agreed. "But when the Huntsman finds Snow White, he's so charmed that he doesn't have the heart to kill her. So he brings the queen the heart of an animal instead. That's why we have the rest of the story of Snow White. Because an assassin lost his nerve."

"So a Starbreaker is a huntsman who never loses his–or her—nerve?"

Jack nodded. "If the evil queen had sent a Starbreaker after Snow White, it would be a cautionary tale of what happens to spoiled brats who wander into the woods alone."

"Destroying the authentic to keep has-beens and wannabes on top," she said, her eyes narrowing with a distinct chill. The woman might be small, but she could pull out some unnerving glares when she was in the mood.

"Basically," he agreed. "You can check with Wanda, but I think she would agree with that description of a Starbreaker."

Nodding like she might indeed follow up with Wanda,

Kali stepped away from him and started weaving her way through the 127 holograms. "What's something else we can look for to catch this Ceravene?"

"Honestly?" Jack replied. "I have no idea. There is no book on Starbreakers."

Kali kept weaving through the rows of possible suspects. "Then how do we even know they still exist? Or that there's one named Ceravene?"

"Because they sign their work," Jack said, his mind recalling the one and only time he'd witnessed a Starbreaker's work ... Ceravene's work, in fact.

It was a memory he could get lost in if he wasn't careful. Best to stay focused on the present.

"How do you know it's really their work?" she asked. "That they're not opportunistically claiming events for their own notoriety?"

"Because the signature appears real-time in the form of a commissioned art piece that depicts their devastation. It's tradition to unveil the piece at an elite gathering or museum the same day."

Her feet paused in their progress as she looked his way. "That's twisted."

"Yes," he replied. "I could ruin some very famous artwork for you if you want a revised history lesson. Before Hollywood came to be what it is, Starbreakers were called Framers because they have the gift of getting the world to collectively see a staged scene while cutting everything else out of the picture."

Kali raised her fingers in air quotes and said, "*I've been framed.*"

"Yes. They are the originators of framing," Jack confirmed.

She started walking again, continuing her tour of holograms.

"But at the end of the day," Jack added, as much for himself as for her, "a Starbreaker ensures someone or something is remembered as the opposite of what it authentically was. They turn potential into a rubble their 'evil queen' of a client can build their pedestal on."

Kali moved to the last line in her tour of suspects. "So we're looking for an expert in human nature … a sociopath with impulse control, who protects their client and is always paying attention to how things appear from a distance."

"Yes," Jack agreed, liking that he was seeing hints of the Kali he'd known before she spent way too long trapped in VR.

Once upon a time, Kali had made a living sniffing out the corrupt, and she'd been very good at it. The look Jack saw sparking in her eyes as she wrapped her mind around their situation reminded him that, while Kali's physical talents were formidable, her inherent talents were mental.

Kali was a Spade—a master of lenses and perspectives, while Jack specialized in currents and appearances. He could really use a mind like Kali's on this if she was offering it. Jack had no desire to admit it out loud, but Kali was smarter than him. She'd just been lurking in shadows and not living up to that part of her potential as of late.

If she wanted to throw ideas at him now, Jack's ears were open.

"How long has Ceravene been around?" she asked him, finishing her tour and returning to his side.

"Ceravene's first signature was spotted eighteen years ago."

"So it's probably someone in their thirties or forties," Kali guessed.

"Unless they were an early- or late-bloomer."

She didn't comment on that. "Does Ceravene move around or have a central location?"

"Signatures have been found in North and South America, along with Europe and South Africa."

She seemed to file that away, too. "Are targets of a type, or do they seem random?"

47

It was a good question, one Jack probably should have answered without prompting. In his defense, he hadn't expected her to be this interested in being helpful.

"Starbreakers like to go down in history books, bedtime stories, and urban legends," Jack replied. "These days, they also like to inspire magazine articles and specials on TV. They aim big with their targets. Always."

She considered that. "They aim big, never miss, and keep their fingerprints off their crime, all while staying off the radar."

"You know as much as I do now."

She arched a skeptical brow at him.

Okay, that wasn't exactly true, but she knew everything that was relevant to possibly catching Ceravene, and enough for her to weigh in if she was feeling helpful.

"How would you smoke out someone who fits that profile?"

Kali let out a bitter laugh. "Me? I'd default to VR Survival 101. To find out who someone is in a scenario, give them a variety of actions to respond to, and watch which ones they mirror."

Jack opened his mouth—ready to say that it wasn't that easy—but paused when her words sparked an idea.

"Ace," he said, angling his voice toward the ceiling. "Let's try a scenario."

All the holograms and projections disappeared, returning the room to a blank slate. *"Ready when you are, Jack."*

3 DAYS LATER

Chapter 5

With a quiet *click*, the final deadbolt on Seba's front door shifted to the unlocked position. Pushing open the door to his studio apartment, he watched the counter embedded in the doorframe click up from 492 to 493, confirming his door hadn't opened since he'd left that morning.

His eyes scanned the room out of habit—from the near wall to the security mirror reflecting the blind spot in the bathroom.

All clear.

He reset the locks—cranking into place the crossbar that could only be set from the inside. Then he stripped off the jacket that had been cooking him all day and headed for the wardrobe against the far wall.

The wardrobe was one of three pieces of furniture in the apartment, along with the extra-long queen-sized bed and a dresser. No pictures. Nothing to steal. If someone did happen to bypass Seba's many layers of security, they would be sorely disappointed with what they found on the other side.

Seba had seen barracks more luxurious.

Opening the wardrobe doors, he slid the false back to the side and stepped through to the neighboring apartment. He was met with a heat wave.

Man, October might only be a week away, but it was still too hot for him to be cheap with the A/C. He should have known as much. If it was too hot outside to be wearing a jacket, it was too warm to leave a sealed-off room fan-less.

The A/C issue Seba could fix, but wearing jackets in the heat was a bullet he would have to keep biting. Los Angeles was not a place where anyone dressed for comfort, if they were looking to get somewhere. The whole city was all about image and status, and Seba needed to look the part wherever he went. It was a job requirement.

The neighboring secret apartment was three times the size of Seba's living space. Once upon a time, the two apartments had been the same size and separate. Seba had knocked down all the walls in both rooms to create a large, open workroom with walled-off windows and doors on one side, and a small studio apartment on the other.

The most valuable item in his apartment was the bed, but his workroom was an entirely different story. The racks of clothes were worth tens of thousands. That didn't include the jewelry or other accessories that could easily sell for over a million dollars, thanks to his forged watch collection.

His industrial equipment and computer systems probably totaled around a hundred grand, although he'd never checked. He'd gotten all of it in trades from clients who hadn't been cash fluid when they'd needed his services.

Trades like that were often preferable to Seba. His clients got what they needed while Seba got off-market equipment, off the books.

Win-win.

Already sweating in the stifling room, Seba undid the buttons of his shirt as he moved to the racks storing his costume wardrobe. He grabbed the log sheet from the wall on his way there and started closing out his work day.

Re-draping the jacket on its coded hanger, Seba checked it in on the log sheet, adding the note that his target had liked the cut and fabric of the jacket and asked who the designer was.

He repeated the process with the rest of his wardrobe for the day—his shirt, belt, pants, rings, watch, and shoes—logging where and when he'd worn them so he could plan accordingly in the future. Then he updated the master sheet, added the shirt to his laundry list, returned the log sheets to their hooks on the wall, and cranked on the A/C—letting it blow on his skin for a few seconds before throwing on some shorts.

A shirt would have to wait until the room actually cooled down.

Busy work done, Seba walked over to check on his latest project: a replica 1794 Flowing Hair dollar coin.

Seba had come across an original on a job the previous week and the owner had let him hold it. So, of course, Seba had swiped a mold of it. There was nothing he loved more than the challenge of creating a perfect forgery. Maybe it stemmed from the first time he'd tried to prize fight when he was fourteen. No one had believed he wasn't at least eighteen. They hadn't let him fight until he got a fake ID that put him in the adult brackets.

Or maybe Seba had been hooked the first time the new fake ID got him out of a winter freeze and into the warmth of an all-night bar where he could play shark at the pool tables to get cash for the next day.

Or maybe the hook had been set the first time he saw a designer bracelet in a window, made a knock-off for twelve bucks, and sold it for fifty. He'd even been upfront about it being fake, but his buyer hadn't cared. She'd said she didn't feel right paying less than fifty.

That's when Seba learned that people didn't really care about what was real.

If a fourteen year old was tall and thick enough, people wanted him to fight with the men. If it was cold outside, a bouncer wanted to see a legit-looking ID and to not have to deal with any trouble. And, if a woman spent too little on something, part of her would always feel cheap in it.

People didn't want reality; they wanted perception. So Seba learned to give people that in exchange for what he wanted: open doors.

A coin like a 1794 Flowing Hair dollar would definitely open some doors. If people asked if it was real, Seba would do what he always did and tell them the truth.

In Seba's experience, that only made them more interested.

People felt more comfortable handling a forgery and wanted to know how he got the detail right and where he'd seen the original. In that way, forgeries often took Seba further than an original ever could when it came to opening doors.

There was more than one way to replicate a coin, but this time around Seba had let his mill do the work while he was off doing other things. The bolted-down square of silver was now buried in silver scrapings that he cleared with a hand-vac before unscrewing the bolts to check out the handiwork against the original mold.

It needed to be sanded into a circle and to have a few hundred years of faux wear-and-tear worked into it, but it was on track to being exactly what he'd seen the week before.

A few more hours work from him and—

Click.

Seba froze at the new sound.

It seemed to have come from the direction of his apartment's front door. Seba knew the sound of every door closing on his floor, but this click had been new and sounded closer.

He set the coin down. Two steps later he was looking down a gun's sites as he silently returned to the portal between apartments.

He paused when his eyes caught sight of his front door. All the deadbolts were in the unlocked position.

Someone was in his apartment. He had no idea how, but that was something to figure out later.

Keeping his head in the game, Seba made quick work of scanning the room from the wardrobe, trigger finger at-the-ready.

He saw nothing.

He didn't hear anything either. No footsteps. No breathing. The neighbor across the hall was cooking, but that was the nearest sound that wasn't coming from Seba himself.

He surged out of hiding, pivoting to face his blind spot the moment he was out of the wardrobe. He spotted an unfamiliar bag and a tri-folded paper on his bed, but sidelined his curiosity to squat down and check under his bed for the intruder.

Clear.

That left the bathroom as the final hiding spot and Seba wasted no time moving that direction. The security mirror was in his blind spot this time around. As Seba stepped through the door frame, gun leading the way, he once again found nothing.

He was alone.

Lowering his gun, Seba walked to his front door and opened it with a simple turn of the knob. When it opened, the counter ticked up from 494 to 495.

Someone had definitely opened it while he was in the other room. But only once.

How had he missed the clank of the crossbar shifting and the other deadbolts clicking open? He should have heard all that long before he heard the soft click of a latch.

It made no sense.

When locked from the inside, the door could only open from the inside. He'd made sure of that. The fact that someone had clearly bypassed his security somehow had Seba feeling like he might be coming down with a sudden case of the flu. His head felt light, his skin too damp, and his heart felt like a captive screaming and banging against his ribs for someone to let it out.

Knowing he had to deal with whatever was on his bed before he made any big decisions, Seba shut and relocked all the deadbolts on the door—including the crossbar—just like he had a few minutes before.

The difference was, a few minutes before, the actions had helped him feel secure. Now it all felt futile.

When he turned to face his bed, he could see the signature band of stacked bills inside a clear plastic bag from his new angle. Tucking the gun into the band of his shorts, Seba took a detour back to his workspace to grab some latex gloves before returning to the bed and picking up the tri-folded paper on top of the money.

The wrapped bills were twenties, which meant he was probably looking at about a hundred grand, if the bills were real.

He left the money where it was and looked at the note.

Dear Seba, it read in fine calligraphy.
A contract has been issued to end the life of Vic Davalos.
We prefer her alive and believe you may, as well. To that end, you will find an advance payment of $100,000 cash to ensure her safety until Saturday at 18:00.
The money is yours to keep whether you accept or reject the offer.
If you accept, know that her internal security and those closest to her cannot be trusted.
If you reject, projections show that Vic Davalos will die by Sunday morning.
The choice is yours.

The letter was signed with a little blue flower, which had to be a seal someone used as their calling card.

Back in New York, Seba had known everyone's seal. He'd even had a rather influential seal of his own. He'd mostly stayed out of the underground scene since moving to

L.A., though, which meant he had no idea what he was looking at or who he was dealing with.

But a little blue flower wasn't his top concern at the moment.

"What is going on?" he whispered to himself, returning to his workroom and going straight for the filing cabinet.

He found the last item he'd filed from pure muscle memory, pulling out a single-page letter he'd received in his PO Box a month before—no prints on the letter and only postal employee prints on the envelope.

Archer,

Next month, an A-list celebrity will require transport from L.A. to an undisclosed location and is in need of a transition team for a total of two weeks.

Pay is $250,000 cash.

You are receiving this offer because of your history of discretion. This will all be off books, with no digital communication.

If interested, please drop a green ball into any underground drop box and we will contact you.

The first letter had no signature.

Seba had declined to respond to the letter in his PO Box. The whole thing smelled like a mess waiting to happen. Anyone who wanted no trail connecting them to someone like Seba was more likely to pay in bullets than bills. That was the main reason Seba did all his transactions through the dark web. The site he used was run by a man who called himself The Broker.

No one double-crossed anyone under The Broker's watch. He held the funds once an agreement was struck and transferred the funds when the job was marked done. The Broker also investigated all user deaths, personally, as part of his fee.

It was a safety net for everyone, so if a client didn't want to subject themselves to that scrutiny, Seba let them shop elsewhere.

But now he had two letters. One said "A-list" and the other said "Vic Davalos" but the timelines for the assignment were the same.

It was too weird to be a coincidence, and probably a trap.

Actually, no *probably* about it. It was definitely a trap. He should do the same thing with the second letter as he'd done with the first. Ignore it.

And yet, murder was different than transporting.

What if the second note was real?

Vic Davalos … dead?

Seba tried to imagine it, but all his mind could drum up was the feel of soft lips against his, followed by a phantom sensation of forgetting his own name.

If life really did flash before someone's eyes at the time of death, Seba wanted any memories of his kiss with Vic Davalos to be part of that slide show.

To this day, he wasn't sure how they ended up locking lips. One moment, he'd been scanning the room for the day's target at a fundraiser. How he'd gone from noticing Vic walk his way to kissing her in the nearby library was still a bit of a blur. But he definitely remembered getting caught, fired, and unceremoniously removed from the event by Evan Bauer's security.

If kissing Vic had been like standing in the sun, getting dragged away was the burn that followed.

Seba could still feel both sensations vividly when he thought about that day: the bask and the burn … the seeing of stars and the sting that followed. The memories were like tattoos he couldn't remove—one a screw up he remembered in vivid detail, while the other was all a blur.

He didn't even know how long they had kissed. Seconds? Minutes? Seba had no clue, and it terrified him. He calculated everything on a job and, with Vic, he'd forgotten how to even count.

Finding himself lost in the memory of the moment yet again, Seba shook himself back to the present and looked at the two letters.

Different penmanship. Different stationery. One had a seal; one was anonymous.

It's none of your business, a voice whispered in the back of his head.

Just because they'd kissed once, it didn't mean it was Seba's job to save Vic. It just meant that his back-pocket memory of them kissing would sour if she actually did die and he'd have a different memory in his slide show when he died.

A memory where he'd shrugged off a threat while she took the fall.

All things considered, that was probably the memory he deserved. It wasn't like he was a good person. When his life flashed before his eyes one day, he knew what he'd see, and it wasn't pretty.

He should forget the letters and keep focusing on himself—starting with a thorough check of his home security measures and how they had failed right under his nose.

Vic could save herself. It was the age of feminism, after all, and every time Vic Davalos popped up on his radar she seemed to be preaching about how women could do anything men could do—only better—and that it was time for women to run the world.

If she was so empowered, let her save herself.

If women wanted to be treated like men, Seba could make that happen. It wasn't like he'd run off to save a male celebrity if someone broke into his home and left a note that the dude's life was in danger.

But ... he would show the guy the notes he'd gotten and let the man decide what to do from there.

"Fine," he mumbled to himself, heading over to his computer while ignoring how his heart started hammering with a new rhythm.

59

"She probably doesn't even remember you," he reminded himself.

With any other woman, such a claim would have sounded self-deprecating. Seba was a good-looking guy. He knew it. But Vic Davalos was around male models every day. Men with muscles had to all blur together at some point in her mind.

Whatever. He'd do this and he'd do it right. Digital trail and all. If something happened to him, at least his disappearance would show up on The Broker's desk. The rest of the world might not notice he was gone until someone tried to tear his apartment building down, but there were a few people on the dark web who were used to trading favors with him that would follow up if he disappeared.

So he'd leave them a trail, starting with his next post on the boards.

ISO>Person>USA>California>LosAngeles
Timeline: *Immediate*
Details: *Seeking current location of Vic Davalos (actual)*
Payment: *$100 USD [IN HOLDING]*

The moment he pressed *Post*, Seba felt an uneasy feeling settle in his stomach.

He was letting himself be played. He could feel it, and yet, he couldn't fight the impatience to get the show on the road as he waited for a response.

He'd kept the payment amount low on purpose. Best to fly low on the radar for the time being. Posting a number that reflected the urgency he felt might attract negative attention and bring others to the scene. If that meant lowballing and having to wait a little bit longer for a response, so be it. He needed to take a shower anyway. He couldn't show up wherever Vic was smelling like a day's worth of sweat. He needed to clean up a bit ... and probably shave again.

Seba was testing his cheek stubble against his hand when

a response came in.

Finder011 can provide ISO location starting at 2300. Click to accept offer.

Finder011? The guy had a perfect record when it came to providing accurate information. Seba had used him more than once and had always gotten what he needed.

Seba clicked *Accept* and a pop-up box opened.

Club Ventis, VIP Lounge. Paid appearance, scheduled start 2300.

Seba knew the club. He'd worked a job there maybe five months ago.

He stood from his chair, grabbing his master log sheet from the wall and scanned the *Location* column until he found *Club Ventis.*

He'd used the alias Kaden Salomon on his last appearance—a rich braggart of a persona who threw around money like he thought he could buy anything. The goal at the time had been to test a man's fiancée to see if she was really in love, or if she would go for an upgrade.

She'd gone for the upgrade and Seba had made quite a show of getting her there, which meant he had to show up as the same man.

Returning the log sheet to the wall, Seba dropped by his computer to verify the response. If it had come from anyone else, Seba would have waited until he actually saw Vic at the club to verify that the information was good. But Finder011 had never led him wrong and he didn't want to insult the guy over a hundred bucks.

Seba had better things to do, and they all started with a shower.

Chapter 6

Vic Davalos loved nothing more than the challenge of creating something one-of-a-kind.

Maybe there really was nothing new under the sun, but Vic was always up for reimagining what the world thought it knew. Especially when it came to fashion.

With Ravel's *Bolero* filling the walls of her design studio, Vic pinned two muslin lapel options on either side of a jacket and stepped back to take a look at her latest design.

Fashion had always been a passion for Vic, but the whole women-in-suits trend really had its hooks in her. The full coverage of the style … the ease of movement … the pockets.

Oh, the pockets—even if it was just a breast pocket that could hold an ID and cash, it would create options so liberating for a woman out on the town. Purses and clutches were a pain, and nothing attracted a thief like a purse.

Whether women-in-suits found its way into the mainstream or not, it was time for pockets to be a mainstay in women's fashion. Vic wanted to be one of the pioneers who made it actually happen.

Unfortunately, according to her manager, Nora, all the polls indicated the look was "off-brand" for Vic to wear personally. The world didn't want a Vic Davalos with full coverage and empowering pockets. They liked her better 60% bare while wearing four-inch heels. So that's what Vic got paid to wear, while a thousand other women nipped at her heels, trying to steal her sponsorships.

Her paychecks would be going to someone else soon enough, but Vic had definitely been hoarding every job that popped up for the past year.

She'd needed to if she had any hope of leaving it all behind.

And in her spare time, like the few hours she'd just found, Vic designed what she'd wear if she had a choice.

She'd always had an eye for what looked good but, when it came to suits, her mind saw all the necessary lines and cuts so clearly ... up until she got to the lapels.

Lapels could make or break a suit, in her opinion. They needed to enhance the silhouette and fabric choices without drawing too much attention to themselves.

Sometimes that meant going big. Sometimes that meant sticking to the classics. Other times it meant embracing the elegant. Every jacket was different so Vic had gotten into the habit over over-cutting the undercollar and lapels of the jacket front, folding them under, and making her final decisions with muslin on a mannequin form.

She'd reached decision time for her latest design: notch, shawl, or cloverleaf lapels?

Vic took a few steps back and held her hands up in a frame to block out all other visual distractions. Then she narrowed the gap so she could only see one side of the jacket at a time.

Notch lapel on the right.

Shawl lapel on the left.

Both had their pros and cons. But when she realized she kept looking at the notch longer and had to force her eyes back to the shawl, she made an executive decision.

Shawl was out.

Bolero crescendoed to its big finish as Vic unpinned the shawl option and replaced it with the cloverleaf. She backed up, holding her hands up for another look, asking, "What would Gal Gadot wear?" to the empty room.

She viewed one side, then the other, picturing Cate Blanchett next ... then Blake Lively ... then Cara Delevingne, noting again that the frame of her hands always held longer on one side.

Cloverleaf it was.

Vic returned to the jacket, removing the notch option and pinning the cloverleaf all the way around to confirm her choice and immediately approved.

A few hours later, the *Queen of the Night* aria filled the room as Vic returned the finished jacket to the mannequin form to check it out. She couldn't fight the smile that tugged at her lips as she took in the final result.

Sometimes Vic gave herself chills with her creations. This was one of those times.

This suit could steal the show on any red carpet. Vic would bet her reputation on it—what little of one that she had.

All the look needed was a few finishing touches, but a glance at the clock revealed they would have to wait until later. Her personal time was up.

It was time to get ready.

Pulling her phone out of her pocket, Vic took several shots of her latest look and shared them to Instagram—not her *official* Instagram. That was run by interns who only posted things that got Vic paid. Nothing personal went on any account with a blue check mark next to it. Everything had to stay on brand.

Besides, posting her hobby to 23 million fans would be cheating anyway. They would like Vic's designs just because she was her. And while that might feel nice, Vic wanted to know if she was genuinely good. She wanted to know she could make it as a designer on her merits, not her connections.

But based on Instagram response to Vic's incognito account, that wouldn't be happening.

Ria's Designs had 1,137 followers, and over 800 of those had followed Vic after she posted contraband behind-the-scenes shots of runway looks during Fashion Week. Most of her followers were more interested in her insider access at large shows than her actual designs. Responses to her actual work usually topped off in the dozens.

It was depressing.

Nora had told her that if she could attract more than 100,000 followers to her designer account, she'd look into packaging Vic as a designer.

Only 99,000 followers to go. But no matter what Vic posted or what hashtags she added, the account stayed as dead as a dance club at noon.

It didn't make sense. Vic had spent most of her life modeling. She knew what was good.

And *she* was good!

When Vic stared at the ceiling at night, she told herself that all she needed to make it was a runway show. The whole world would see the real her and want more.

Maybe in her next life.

Vic smiled at the thought but didn't want to jinx herself by daydreaming too much. Someone might catch her.

She needed to march along like everything was business as usual, wearing sponsored clothes to sponsored events and putting money in the bank while she still could.

Come Sunday, she'd be making her last withdrawal so now was the time to get her game face on and her nest egg coming in.

Luckily, her hair was night-ready. All she had to do was slap a night look on her face, get her sponsored look on, and she'd be good to go.

Twenty minutes later, Vic noted that the hem of that night's skirt was happy to slide up her butt cheeks as she leaned over to fasten her heels. She was going to have to be careful moving around. This little number was a creeper.

She fought the clasps on the shoes a bit, finally punched a new hole in each side that kept them from being so loose that they drooped or so tight they bit in.

In three days, you'll never have to deal with crappy shoes again. You can wear anything you want, she reminded herself, standing to check out the final look in the mirror.

"Ow!" she breathed, immediately sitting back down and trying to fix the stab she felt behind her ankle. It felt like a sharp piece of plastic gouging into her Achilles, making it impossible to take a normal step.

"What's your deal?" she asked the shoe as she inspected it.

A few moments later, she found its fatal flaw: cheap materials.

Nothing was poking out. The cut of the heel piece just didn't flex.

Vic reached for her phone.

Tonight's shoes are unwearable, she texted Nora. *Give the sponsor a refund. I have the film shoot tomorrow. I can't sever my Achilles tonight.*

She crossed her fingers for Nora to agree with her as she put her phone back down and removed the shoes. Then she stood, taking a look in the mirror, one hand toying with her mother's necklace as she decided boots might work with the skirt.

Her phone chimed with a text.

Nora: Can you make them work?

No can do. They're cutting me, Vic typed back, adding some sad emojis after.

Nora: The sponsor won't be pleased.

That was code for: *Evan owned the company.*

But Vic couldn't even stand up straight without feeling like she might be doing permanent damage. She couldn't dance in shoes like that all night. It was an impossibility.

Decision time. If she didn't wear the shoes, Evan would not be pleased, but would he even find out before Sunday?

Sorry, she replied, deliberately ditching the phone so she wouldn't have to see any reply as she headed to her closet to choose some boots.

Her eyes landed on a pair of hand-painted cowboy boots she'd never gotten to wear out. They were a nice, playful touch to an otherwise slutty look … a bit of a girl-next-door-gone-wild vibe when she smiled.

The remaining sponsors should be pleased.

Grabbing the night's clutch—empty, save for the stuffing that shaped it into photographable perfection—Vic took one last glance in the mirror before noting the time. If they left right now, they might even arrive a few minutes early and make sure the manager was happy so that Nora only had one unhappy call to handle tomorrow.

Turning off the bathroom light, Vic started for the main part of the house, where Tristan and Bret were waiting for her.

"Stop."

It was the voice, not the word, that got Vic freezing in place. Everything else still, her eyes moved to the foot of her bed where her step-father stood.

His eyes looked her up then back down, making a pointed landing on her boots. "Don't tell me you're leaving like that."

Chapter 7

Deep bass pulsed through the club's windows and two doors, filling the street with a surging hum that beckoned the world to its party.

Outside the entrance, Vic posed for the cameras in front of the night's sponsor wall. Professional photographers clicked away on the other side of a red rope while club-goers waiting in the general admission queue snapped their own photos when they had a good angle.

"Over here, Vic!" one photographer called out, taking multiple shots in a gamble that she'd look his way.

She didn't.

"How about a little bend?" urged another.

"Smile, baby," yelled another. "Why so mad?"

Vic ignored them all, moving through her signature poses as the backs of her high heels threatened to saw her feet off at the ankles.

At least it's warm, she told herself while flipping a mental bird to all the cameras.

That was her *signature*-signature look. Her moneymaker.

And it was all theirs.

When the camera shutters started clicking triple-time, Vic decided to call it quits while she was on top.

A pinch of pain had her faltering a little on her first step as her brain underestimated the upgrade in pain management. Hopefully, it passed for a tipsy wobble.

"Where are you going, honey?" a photographer yelled on the second step and was quickly joined with a chorus of other voices yelling different versions of the same before cameras started going crazy again to get images of her walking away.

Six more steps to freedom ... five more steps ... four more steps—

"Welcome to Club Ventis, Ms. Davalos," the VIP doorman said, a light blush coloring his cheeks over an otherwise professional smile as he opened the rope for her.

"Hey, Tyson," she said, getting his name off the nametag on his chest.

His blush deepened. "Thank you, Ms. Davalos."

Thank you, for what? Saying his name? For some reason, his reaction was almost enough to help her forget about her shoe situation.

Almost.

Three more steps—she reached the threshold of the entrance—*two more steps*—the bass of EDM music surrounded her as one foot stepped through the door—*last step.*

Freedom!

White light pulsed from the stage while neon lasers wove in and out of linear designs in the darkness.

For a moment, Vic couldn't see anything but the bright lights against the black of the club. Then Tristan stepped in next to her, urging her forward, but she forced herself to a stop just as a female VIP escort stepped forward to greet her.

"Hi, Ms.—"

Vic motioned for the escort to hold her thought before using the entrance wall as cover while she bent over and rid herself of the shoes.

With one shoe off and one to go, Tristan leaned over and whispered in her ear, "Are you sure this is wise?"

"Add it to your list," she replied through gritted teeth.

Tristan straightened, making a noise like he disapproved as Vic used the flashing lights to take note of the dark stripes across the back of her ankles.

"Are you okay, Ms. Davalos?" the escort asked, getting Vic to look up.

The woman couldn't have been any older than Vic, which always made formal greetings a bit more awkward.

"Better now," Vic yelled over the music. "Where's the bar?"

"Right this way, Ms. Davalos."

As they made their way to a second set of velvet ropes, Vic gave Tristan's arm a little tap before pointing to her ears. He responded by pulling her phone and ear plugs out of his breast pocket and handing them over. Then Vic crossed into the VIP area and left Tristan to join Bret in a private security lounge where they could watch her on cameras.

Happily, Ventis management didn't like the vibe of a VIP station that was half-filled with stern-looking security. It wasn't really their thing.

It wasn't Vic's either.

Tucking the ear plugs into her bra for later, Vic followed the escort to the VIP area. She heard someone shout her name somewhere in the crowd but didn't stray from her path to the bar. It was pretty much abandoned this early in the night. Everyone seemed invested in claiming booths, tables, or the dance floor over the obvious pick-up zone.

Perfect.

"Two shots, two glasses," she yelled to the sassy-haired bartender. "Bacardi 151."

The bartender nodded—one hand reaching up for the desired bottle while the other palmed two fresh glasses and set them up for the pour. Vic leaned up against the bar and waited, reminded by the airflow from behind that her skirt could not be trusted to behave tonight.

Well, that makes two of us, Vic thought as she plopped

her shoes down on the bar and tucked her phone into the back of her skirt.

The escort leaned in, her face flashing in the strobing white light. "If there is anything I can get you, Ms. Davalos, please let me know."

"A lighter?" Vic said, pantomiming flicking one, in case she couldn't be heard.

The girl understood, pulling one from her jacket. "I can show you the smoking lounge, if you'd like to follow me."

Vic shook her head and plucked the lighter from the girl's hand. When Vic motioned for her to step back as well, the escort looked confused, but complied.

When Vic turned back to the bar, the shots were waiting for her. She picked up one shot in each hand, poured them over the shoes, and flicked the lighter to life. Then she got out of the way quickly as the shoes burst into a blaze.

The bartender's eyebrows shot up with surprise, but not alarm. This wasn't the bar's first fire trick. Maybe just its first trick involving flaming shoes.

Behind Vic, a shout of approval rose up from the crowd. They were still cheering the flame on when the bartender pulled a hooked instrument off the wall and grabbed a large ice bucket.

An unceremonious swipe of the hook later, the cursed shoes fell into the bucket and were covered by a lid, leaving only the smell of burning plastic behind.

Off to Vic's side, her escort looked like she didn't know what to do next. But the bartender did.

Spraying an aerosol to neutralize the reek of the shoes, she sent Vic a smile, "Girl, we've all been there."

That seemed to wake up her escort. "Will you be needing another pair of shoes, Ms. Davalos?"

"Yes," Vic replied, handing the lighter back. "Size seven-and-a-half."

The escort cut out to find new shoes as a flood of clubbers surrounded Vic, offering to buy her next drink.

The party was officially on.

Chapter 8

Everyone in the club moved in snapshots of white light, timed to the deafening beat of a song that repeated the same hook on a loop. The flicker of the strobe was enough for Seba to see what he needed to see from the main bar opposite the VIP lounge.

Unless someone could die of popularity, Vic Davalos was doing fine. That was Seba's assessment from the far-side of Club Ventis.

She was safe, but that had nothing to do with any of the guards she'd come in with. They were crap, that was for sure. They hadn't even pretended to check the environment for threats. They were just big dudes in suits who didn't smile at anything.

They were deterrents, not protection.

For all Seba knew, the two guys who came in with her were just models posing as guards until they got their next gig. Getting past them would be a cake walk for a professional killer.

The question was, who would want Vic dead? Her competition? Someone powerful with a secret to hide?

Or was Seba the one being played in this whole thing? Was he being lured into something? Was Vic Davalos some kind of bait being used to keep his attention while someone snuck up on him?

Was he the dupe?

No, he thought, taking a sip of scotch as he watched Vic take a selfie with some dude who pressed a kiss to her cheek at the last moment. Vic laughed at the move, throwing her head back as the guy's eyes dropped down. Seba fought the urge to rub the stress out of his neck as he mulled over the situation.

It made no sense to use Vic as bait to set him up. Two years, three months, and seventeen days ago, he'd spent a total of five-ish minutes of his life with her. They hadn't even been on the same city block since that day. There was no reason for anyone in the world to believe they had a connection.

So why had he gotten two letters about her? It didn't make sense. None of it did.

When the flashing lights showed Vic dancing again—arms wrapped around her as she moved—Seba downed the rest of the scotch and forced himself to do another scan of the room.

Plenty of wolves were hunting that night but, so far, the sheep looked willing enough. Everyone was lost in their own world except one guy. He had been staring at Vic the last time Seba had looked his way.

Blue shirt … mama-boy haircut … maybe five-foot-ten. He watched Vic as if fantasizing about what he'd do if he was one of the people currently surrounding her.

In a room that pulsed with motion, Blue Shirt stood still. Fixated. Or maybe the better word was entranced. Either way, he had the signature mannerisms of someone with the potential to be problematic.

People looking to stir trouble rarely blended. They were either too still or too manic in comparison to the people around them. This guy was one of the still, unblinking ones. He made the same picture every time the lights flashed, eyes locked wherever Vic stood—body tense and respirations shallow, which meant his heart rate had to be elevated. Instinct told Seba the man had come to the club that night *just* to see Vic. He certainly hadn't dressed to fit in.

Probably a stalker to some degree.

Seba looked away, scanning the crowd again—this time, like a man on the prowl. He caught a pair of eyes looking back his way from the dance floor. A woman. Brunette. Beautiful. She smiled his way and gestured for him to join her.

That was his cue.

As much as people noticed someone like Blue Shirt in a crowd, they also noticed the broody guy hanging out at the bar, giving all the hot women a cold shoulder. Men like that stood out more than the blue shirts.

It was time to play his part—blending in and dropping cash on the ladies—until Vic made her exit. Someone needed to watch to see who followed her, and based on what Seba had seen so far, it wasn't going to be her security team.

Chapter 9

The moon smiled like a Cheshire cat in the night sky as Seba rapped his knuckles against the steel shutters covering a business entrance for the night.

A shotgun cocked on the other side of the metal.

"It's Archer," Seba said.

A moment later, the latch released and the base and shutters rolled up.

"These aren't your usual business hours," DHack said, motioning for Seba to come in as his eyes swept the background for anyone watching. There was no one. Seba had made sure of that.

"Nothing about this job is usual," Seba replied, stepping in so DHack could drop the shutters again.

"Unusual is what I'm paid for," DHack said, sliding the latch back into place before turning to Seba. "Whadda ya' got?"

Seba held up a foil packet. "I cloned four phones and I need you to tell me what I'm dealing with."

"My fee?"

Seba held up a second envelope.

DHack smiled and gestured toward the EMPLOYEES ONLY entrance of the high-end electronics store. If there was a gig in L.A., DHack had the equipment, trucks, and staff to run it. On the side of doing all that, DHack was a programming genius. The guy might have been only in his late twenties and look like he belonged in a heavy metal band, but he knew programming like no one else Seba had ever met.

"Let's head to the dark room, shall we?" he said.

Seba nodded and followed the man to the back office. Behind the office was a room that blocked all external signals to keep everything inside contained.

Seba handed the man both envelopes and let him get to work.

After a glance in the money envelope, DHack opened the foil envelope and slid out four smartphones, taking note of Seba's labels.

"Okay," DHack said, flipping them label-up. "Looks like we've got two guards, a target, and a stalker."

Seba nodded. "I don't expect any problems with the stalker phone, but the other three might be running something top-tier in the background. I need you to tell me what I'm dealing with and how it could flag me."

DHack nodded. "Cool. Let's start with the target."

Seba leaned against the wall and gave the guy some silence to work in as he logged into a computer, found the right adapter for the phone and connected it. Code started populating the screen faster than the eye could follow. When it finished, DHack deployed his programs to weave their way through all the code and pop up what they flagged in separate windows.

When one of the windows popped up pulsing red, DHack groaned. "I should have charged you more. I need to buy a new computer now."

Seba pushed away from the wall. "Why?"

DHack started clicking through the pop ups, his eyes seeming to discern the code at a glance. "That is a question with a multi-faceted answer. Give me a second."

Doing his best not to hover, Seba waited for DHack to do what he needed to do.

"You're not dealing with top-tier here," he said. "You're dealing with: totally off-market."

"So maybe you owe me for this one?" Seba joked.

DHack jerked his thumb toward the computer. "So long as this baby is never connected to anything that sees the light of day again, maybe. I can't give any of the phones back to you." He tapped the clone of Vic's phone. "There's a beaconing virus on here designed to narc on anything the parent phone touches. It flares like a supernova when it feels threatened, pirating anything it touches to help send a signal back to home base tattling on who offended them and how."

"Whoa," Seba said, needing a second to process that.

"Yeah. And that's just the tip of the iceberg so far. Do you have any other phones on you right now?"

Seba shook his head. "I only had the four and I put them all in the envelope back at the club."

"Good move," he said. "Maybe there's a chance I won't be meeting men in black tomorrow."

Seba felt his heart pump nervously. "It's that serious?"

"I know some government spies who would kill for half of what's going on here," DHack said. "And, no, that's not a metaphor. They would actually kill."

"For what, exactly?" Seba said, leaning in to look at the code. He knew basics, but not enough to read it like DHack could.

"Figuring that out will take some time," he said, turning back to look at the screen.

"What can you tell me now?" Seba asked.

"A lot of these programs are standard. The phone acts as a microphone in any room it's in; the GPS is always broadcasting, and all behavior is monitored. Blah, blah, blah. One interesting thing I'm seeing is how the functionality of apps is controlled."

"By doing what?"

DHack brought one of the windows to the front. "Like this is a program that interfaces with Instagram. Whenever the app is opened, the program changes the user status to Public. Whenever the app closes, the profile and posts are all switched to Private."

"Why would there be a program for something like that?" Seba asked.

DHack shrugged. "No clue. But that's one of the custom bits. Haven't seen this exact coding before today." He looked up at Seba. "Any idea who developed it."

"Maybe Evan Bauer," Seba said, more interested in maintaining a good relationship than keeping a secret. "At least, that's where the trail starts."

"Really?"

Seba nodded.

"That's … a pretty big deal, actually," DHack said, eyes staring off at nothing for a moment as he seemed to weigh the implications.

"Why?" Seba asked.

"Because Bauer's laying low and playing small in this arena," DHack said, his brain still clearly crunching through the revelation. "But with the kind of spyware I'm seeing here, he can pirate phones like spreading yawns in a room. And any phone that doesn't yawn along probably belongs to a sociopath."

Seba seriously hated technology. Every time he turned around, tech seemed to be selling him out. That's why he switched phones between each job and never stored anything on them.

Too risky.

"But we're safe right now?" he asked.

DHack hesitated and nodded. "So long as you really put these in the foil envelope at the club, probably, yes."

Seba nodded. "I cloned and stowed them right away."

"Okay. So you weren't tracked here, but Mama Hen server knows what you've done and she's waiting for her cloned baby to see the light of day and start chirping for her to come find it." He pointed to a hatch on the wall. "And that's why all four of these phones are going in the incinerator before you leave, and why nothing else can touch this computer for as long as it lives. They are all hardwired snitches now with a virus that is meant to be passed until Mama has everyone back where they belong."

Unreal. "It's that advanced?"

DHack nodded. "It's only a few steps away from being an AI, but I think that's intentional. I think the designer doesn't want to deal with something capable of thinking for itself."

Yep. Sounded like Evan Bauer's style.

Seba pointed to the phone. "What does it do instead of think?"

"It monitors," DHack said, starting to click through the windows. "Pretty much everything. Movement patterns, speed of movement, heart rate, phone engagement." He stopped on one of the windows and pointed to the indecipherable code. "I mean, this protocol right here sends a flare up to Mama if heart rate goes above 120 or below 40."

Why 120? That wasn't very high. A fast walk, maybe. Why flag something like that?

"I could spend hours going into all the details," DHack said. "But, basically, this phone is Big Brother, recording real-time and tattling on everything. Even breathing. If it has a signal, it's talking."

"No way to stop it?"

DHack shrugged. "I've got a signal disrupter I can sell you, if you like, but Mama also tracks all the missing time when her babies can't be reached. Where? When? How long? All that. You can use a disrupter, but Mama will know and send messages to help daddy—probably Bauer, in this case— resolve the issue."

What a headache. Sometimes Seba really understood Luddites.

"Is it just with this phone?" he asked. "Or the others,

too?"

DHack unhooked the clone of Vic's phone and plugged in the first guard phone, repeating the scanning process.

"Different parameters ... fewer programs running but this phone is tracked by the same system, yes."

He plugged in the next and, thirty seconds later, said, "Same."

"Insane," Seba muttered.

DHack held up the last phone. "And this stalker phone? Anyone sophisticated?"

Seba shook his head. "Just someone with an unhealthy crush, from what I can tell."

DHack nodded. "Well, the phone will be infected when I plug it into this computer, but I should be able to get a read on it before it's overwritten."

"That's good enough," Seba said.

The program ran, and this time only a few windows popped up.

"Yeah," DHack confirmed, clicking through the code. "Only corporations are spying on this guy. Standard stuff here—whoa. Wait. Maybe not."

"What?"

DHack held up his hand for silence as he leaned forward and examined some code that didn't even use the Latin alphabet. It was all symbols.

"That looks different from the other code we were looking at," Seba pointed out.

"It is," DHack confirmed. "It's ..."

He copied the code and opened another program—an audio one, by the looks of it. After fiddling a bit, he got something to play. Or, at least, a sound graph on the screen said it played something, but Seba couldn't hear anything.

"Can we turn the audio up?"

"It's up," DHack said, pointing to the graph like Seba was supposed to understand what it was indicating. "It's playing an inaudible frequency—out of range for human ears."

"Why would something like that be installed?"

DHack sent him a look. "Don't ask questions like that unless you want me to put my tinfoil hat on."

"Got it," Seba said. To him, this was all tinfoil talk. Tech wasn't his scene. He was street, not geek. "How about the basic answer? Why would a phone be programmed to play an inaudible frequency."

DHack shrugged. "All I can tell you is that this code is programmed to play when a certain media tag is accessed."

"Can you tell what the tag is?" Seba asked.

DHack shook his head. "Don't know this code. I'd have to see what activates it to really know. And since this phone can never see the light of day again, it would have to be saved on the phone."

Seba stepped forward, swiping the phone awake and navigating to the Download files. It was like a gallery of everything Vic Davalos. From her looking innocent, to her looking far from it.

Seba clicked on one of the tamer images. "How about this?"

The sound graph on the screen started pulsing as the sound file played and looped.

"We have a winner," DHack said.

Seba tilted his head and tried to listen. "The sound is playing right now?"

"It is. Just out of our hearing range."

Seba held still. "Should I be noticing something?"

"Maybe not after ten seconds. But you might unconsciously react over time. You might get a headache, for example, and not know why."

Seba had actually experienced that.

"Although," DHack amended. "If the guy is stalking her, and not running away, my guess is that it might be a frequency that tickles the reward center of the brain. But that's tinfoil talk creeping through. Point is: the code's installed, it plays when it's asked, and, according to you, the phone's owner is stalking the source material tagged to the frequency. Use that information however you will, but know that the guy's phone is normal when it comes to everything else."

It was a lot to process. Seba had brought the phones over to try to avoid trip wires in trailing her only to find out that all digital options were off the table.

He'd have to go old school on this, which maybe wasn't the worst thing ever.

"Do you still have those two-way radios that look like cell phones?"

DHack nodded. "Sure do. I can ring you up out front."

"Sweet. I'll need two modifications, plus that jammer you mentioned."

"Sure," DHack said, picking up the phones and carrying them to the incinerator. "You're the boss."

Chapter 10

Vic was resting her eyes, wishing she was still back in bed, when the SUV came to a stop.

"We're here," Ryan said a beat before a valet opened Vic's door.

"Good morning, Ms. Davalos," the hotel employee said, looking quite chipper for eight in the morning. But Vic was running on four hours of sleep.

"Morning," she managed, grateful not to hear any cameras clicking as she swung her legs out of the SUV. The production company had lived up to its word of keeping the site paparazzi-free, it seemed. Happy day.

"Please check in at the front desk," the valet said, offering his hand for balance as Vic exited the vehicle. "They'll have the keys to your private room for breaks."

"Thank you," Vic said, as Ryan appeared from around the back of the SUV to escort her inside the hotel.

They'd be filming on the rooftop lounge and pool area. Vic would be playing the arm candy girl who couldn't decide if she was more attracted to the ugly villain's money or the hero's hotness.

Deep stuff.

But, whatever. It wasn't like she was an actor with a huge

range. Best to stick with her strengths.

Besides, this would be her last role. She'd never have to spend another day on a film set again. She might never even be in a hotel like this again—watching people weave through a busy lobby on their way to somewhere. Power suits criss-crossing with business-length skirts, while people dressed in all black—probably part of the film crew—argued on their phones about things apparently not going to plan.

For as much as Vic hated large cities, she was pretty sure she would miss the buzz of energy that came from living in one.

"You look tired," Ryan said from next to her. "There's a smoothie shop down the street. Want me to grab you something?"

He was being nice for some reason. It was hard not to be suspicious.

"A turmeric smoothie would be awesome," she said as they reached the front desk. Four hours wasn't enough sleep for her. She had to perk up somehow.

"Welcome, Ms. Davalos," the attendant said, sliding an envelope across the counter as Vic stole a glance at her nametag. "You are all checked in. These are the keys to your room."

"Thanks, Leticia" Vic said, noting the room number and handing one of the keycards over to Ryan. "Someone is supposed to swing by the room and take me to makeup in twenty minutes."

He looked around the lobby. "I should probably go up with you before I make the run."

Vic shrugged. "Everyone here is a guest or part of the movie. I'll be fine."

He took the card. "Okay. Be right back."

Then he headed back out the way they came, her phone still stowed in his pocket. She should have called him back and asked for it.

She didn't.

Taking her first deep breath of the day, Vic headed for the elevators. The first one was loaded with production equipment and the next had a group of men in it, so she waited for the third one to ding and slide open. Two women stepped out, one of them giving Vic a double-take—seeming to recognize her even when Vic tilted down the brim of her hat while stepping into the elevator.

Luckily, the woman didn't stop. It was too early for cameras. All Vic wanted to do was get to her room and lay down until makeup came for her.

If she was lucky, they were running behind.

Vic punched the button for the eighth floor and gave a little thanks to the universe when the elevator doors glided shut with only her inside.

She leaned against the sidewall on the ride up, letting her head rest against the wall and her eyes drift shut and didn't open them again until the elevator gave a little ding.

Her eyes opened almost as slowly as the doors and she got her feet moving, following the signs until she found her door. A slide of a card later, the lock flashed green and she pushed into the room.

The first thing she saw were the curtains—a terrible mix of yellow, white, and grey. The rest wasn't so bad, she decided, as she walked down the short hall to the main room. Two lounge chairs—white and grey—a large-screen TV, a platform bed with a comforter that needed to disappear, and, on the other side of that, a thickly muscled man leaning against the far wall.

A man she'd seen before.

A man she'd kissed before.

A man who definitely wasn't supposed to be there.

"Hi, Vic," he said, not moving. "Remember me?"

Chapter 11

Vic wasn't drowsy anymore. She was wide awake as she noted the fact that the man she'd spent way too many hours daydreaming about was taller than she remembered. And thicker. And his hair was definitely shorter.

The last time she'd seen him, it had been long enough for her to tangle her fingers into and hold on. Now it was all a uniform buzz.

It shouldn't have looked good. It did.

It *so* did.

Just like his un-arched eyebrows shouldn't be sexy. They should have made him look like a Neanderthal, or some perpetually pissed-off cartoon character. Instead, he looked like he had a direct view into her soul and knew every lie she'd ever told.

They're just eyebrows, she reminded herself.

Maybe it was the sharp chisel of his jaw line that made the no-nonsense brow work. Whatever the case, they channeled the blue of his eyes into a perpetual smolder.

A smolder aimed right at Vic as he waited for her to recover from her shock and answer his question.

Vic's eyes flitted to the door, knowing she could get out of the room in a few steps if she tried. But she wasn't scared for some reason. She was somewhere between excited and curious as she replied.

"Yes. I don't tend to kiss and forget."

Straightening, he stepped away from the wall. "Well, that's something, at least."

What was that supposed to mean?

Also, had his hands always been that big? Because Vic felt like she would have remembered hands that could palm her face like a basketball. Maybe it was the enclosed space or adrenaline that was making everything about him seem larger than she remembered.

"Let me state the obvious and say I should not be here," the man said.

"Uh, yeah," Vic replied, finally finding her attitude. "What are you doing here?"

"I'm here because your personal security sucks," he said, tipping his chin in the direction of the door. "Whatever loser you have with you today should have cleared the room before you entered."

Vic rolled her eyes. "He's grabbing me a smoothie."

Sparkling blue eyes glared at her under flat brows. "Not his job. His job is to check the room. And everywhere else, for that matter."

"Well, maybe he will from now on, if you're going to be a crazy stalker."

When he took a step forward, a voice in the back of Vic's head whispered she should be scared ... or screaming ... or calling Ryan to forget the smoothie and run up to throw this guy out.

Not that he could.

But it was Ryan's job to try, and Vic should be sounding an alarm. Instead, she held her ground as the man took a step toward her.

"I'm here because something has come to my attention."

She heard the words Mr. Muscles was saying. They even made sense. But something about him being one step closer made her brain go on the fritz a bit, making it difficult to really comprehend them.

Which was why the only response her mind could think to drum up was an inelegant, "Yeah?"

Another step. "Yeah."

Whoa. Vic needed him to stop right there or this whole creepy situation would turn into Library Make Out 2.0, and she was due in makeup in fifteen-ish minutes. She didn't need anyone walking in on a TMZ moment.

It was while thinking of cameras and "sources close to the couple" that Vic figured out how to work her brain again.

"What are you doing here?" she asked.

It was the first question she should have asked him. Better late than never.

Something flickered in his smolder. "I'm here to give you a heads up. I got two anonymous offers to work for you this weekend. Know anything about that?"

What? Vic knew the answer was written on her face, but she answered anyway. "No."

He held the left side of his jacket open to show her papers folded in his breast pocket before reaching over to pull them out with his right hand. "I got the first offer a month ago, and the second yesterday. I'd like you to see them."

Something in his tone had nerves prickling up the back of Vic's neck, but she didn't let it show. "Okay, I guess."

He closed the distance between them—the scent of his cologne coming in range, one she didn't recognize but was definitely going to find later—and handed her the first paper.

Vic tried to read it with a poker face, but knew for a fact her expression faltered when she saw the first line.

Archer,

Next month, an A-list celebrity will require transport from L.A. to an undisclosed location and is in need of a transition team for a total of two weeks.

Pay is $250,000 cash.

You are receiving this offer because of your history of discretion. This job will all be off books, with no digital communication.

If interested, please drop a green ball into any underground drop box and we will contact you.

Vic felt her heart pick up in panic. The details were uncomfortably accurate to her situation. Come Saturday, she would be flying somewhere, and she did have a transition team.

But this guy couldn't know that.

No one but Nora knew and they'd been very careful to keep it that way. And keeping that secret had depended highly on playing it cool when confrontations like this happened.

So Vic looked up from the letter. "Archer?"

The guy flinched as if he'd forgotten that part was there, but recovered quickly. "It's my handle when people hire me."

"Like when my step-father hired you?"

The man gave a terse nod. "Yes. Anyway, I thought you might find the rest of the note a bit more interesting."

Vic shrugged. "Nothing here mentions me. It could be talking about anyone."

"True," he agreed, holding out the second paper. "I had no idea the job was related to you until I got this letter."

Dear Seba,

A contract has been issued to end the life of Vic Davalos.

We prefer her alive and believe you may, as well. To that end, you will find an advance payment of $100,000 cash to ensure her safety until Saturday at 18:00.

The money is yours to keep whether you accept or reject the offer.

If you accept, know that her internal security and those closest to her should not be trusted.

If you reject, projections show that Vic Davalos will die

by Sunday morning.
The choice is yours.

"Seba," she said, testing the name on her lips as she looked up. "Is that your name?"

"Again, not the point," he said, looking more than a little flustered. "It's the rest of the letter I'm here to talk about."

It was. His name was totally Seba.

Was that short for something?

"I thought you might be more interested in the—"

"—vast amounts of money people are apparently willing to pay you for a few days work?" Vic finished for him. "Because, I have to say, that even I don't command that much very often."

He plucked the letters from her hand, his body radiating angry heat as he held them up for her to see. "Forget my name, forget the money, and look at this! Did you miss the part that talks about you being dead by Sunday?"

No. She hadn't. But she also understood how a letter like that might have been written.

It meant she'd screwed up somewhere.

What Vic didn't know was how it had brought the man-who-got-away back to her door three days before she planned on leaving forever.

Talk about terrible timing.

How many times had she dreamed of this guy showing up again? How many times had she looked for him, or wished to trade him out for the person she was with?

Now here he was. Right when she was making a run for it, he shows up and she learns his name.

Seba.

Man, life really was what happened when you were making other plans. ... but whatever. They'd missed their window. There was only one thing to do about it now.

"Look," she said. "Whoever wrote that second letter probably had the best of intentions, but they're missing some facts. And whoever wrote you that first letter" —Nora— "definitely didn't do so under my direction." Or get her permission on the offered amount.

A quarter-million for two weeks' work? What was this guy's going rate? And what did he do to earn it? That was insane … although numbers like that might explain his wardrobe. Vic was pretty sure his shirt was Prada.

Seba—the name was really growing on her—frowned at her. "So you're 100% sure that I'm not going to wake up on Sunday to news that you died overnight?"

Oooh. Trick question.

Vic opened her mouth to assure him she would be fine and found herself struggling for an answer. His question was too direct for one of her usual work arounds. And, for some reason, she didn't want to lie.

Would he wake up to news that she had died? Yes.

Would she be dead? No.

"No one's going to be killing me this weekend," she promised, her stomach turning when she realized he wouldn't see it that way when he woke up Sunday morning.

What if he felt guilty about not warning her enough and sniffed around? What if he was good at sniffing around?

He might undo everything.

"How can you be certain?" he pushed and something flashed in his eyes that got Vic making a split-second decision.

"No one's planning to kill me on Saturday," she confessed. "I'm killing me."

Chapter 12

Seba felt his heart stall in his chest as shock washed through him. He couldn't help but look her over, taking in the beauty every instinct in him was willing to stand in line to take a bullet for.

Aquamarine eyes that met his with startling clarity … skin so smooth only marble could feign to capture its texture, but never its warmth … lips that sparked memories of the first time in his life he'd felt like all the dark in his life might actually have an opposite.

And she was standing there—with a straight face—telling him that she was thinking of … no! He must have misheard.

"What?" he asked, unable to keep the incredulity out of his voice.

Vic seemed to grow immediately flustered. "I mean, not literally. I won't be *killing*-killing myself," she modified. "Just … disappearing forever by leaving behind a plane crashed in the ocean with no bodies recovered."

It took a lot to surprise Seba. He couldn't even remember the last time it had happened. But Vic Davalos's confession had him reeling.

"You're going to fake your own death?"

Vic looked as surprised that she'd said it as he'd been to

hear it when she stabbed a finger his way. "You can't tell anyone. I don't even know why I told you. Temporary insanity, maybe? I just don't want you to wake up on Sunday and think you should have tried harder to convince me I was in trouble or something."

Seba couldn't tell if he felt nothing or was too angry to feel. "You don't want *me* to feel bad?"

"No," she said emphatically, her perfect face somehow managing to look innocent. "Of course not!"

Mad. He was definitely mad. "What about everyone else? Friends? Fans? People who actually know you? Don't you care how they feel?"

She had the nerve to wave that concern off. "There will be a couple days of posting memes and selfies people took with me, and maybe a couple weeks of nostalgic sales for my sponsors. But my fans are all about having fun. And grieving isn't fun. So everyone will move on quickly. There are a dozen girls who will be jockeying to take my spot by the end of the week. Just watch."

She'd thought about this, Seba realized. A lot. And not from a glass-half-full space. Vic's smile might be bright enough to light up a room, but it was a light she gave, not a light she felt.

She honestly believed no one would really care if she disappeared.

How could she be so blind?

Seba shook his head. "What's the point? If you're legally dead, all you've worked for—all your money and assets— disappears."

For the first time, her eyes couldn't meet his. They shimmered with regret before dropping. "I know. But I have a way to keep some of it."

Was she kidding? "Then there's the fact you have one of the most recognizable faces in America—"

"Which is why I'm leaving the continent," she countered.

"Why?" Seba hadn't meant to yell it. He didn't even

know why he cared. But apparently he did.

People didn't walk around throwing away their life's work. It made no sense.

"Are you in legal trouble?" he pressed, thinking of her phone but wanting her to guide the conversation. He already knew what he knew. He needed to know what she was looking at in all of this. "Are you being blackmailed? Do you need help?"

"No," she replied, motioning for him to quiet his voice. "Nothing like that, okay? Not that it's any of your business—"

"Then help me understand," he said, squaring off in front of her. "You have everything a person could want in your hands. Why cut it all off and run?"

The laugh that answered him was bitter. And when Vic made her reply, her tone was ice cold. "I don't expect you to understand."

"Why not try me anyway?" he snapped back, not willing to let it go even though he should have been out the door long ago. "I might understand more than you think."

Vic laughed like she doubted that was possible, so he pushed harder.

"You've had everything from birth," he said in a jeering tone that always got under people's skins. "Your parents were icons who *had* to have left you a massive inheritance. On top of that, you were adopted by billionaires who raised you with every privilege known to man. And now you get paid just to be seen! There are people out there who would kill to be you. And you're going to fake a plane crash to escape it?"

This time her eyes were as cold as her voice. "My parents loved drugs more than me. I was adopted by people who needed some positive PR to save their companies. And I've had zero control over my life since I became a full-time model when I was fourteen. I didn't ask for any of this."

"So quit! Move on, like everyone else in the world. Do

something else."

"I. Can't," she said, voice hushed, but intense. "I can't even move out of the Bauer's place. Everywhere I try to go, all it takes is one call from Evan Bauer to get me blacklisted. The way he sees it, I owe him and have since the day he adopted me. So now I'm a walking billboard for his crappy companies while he controls my image, my reputation, and all the money. And I'm sick of it, okay? I'm done being his slave!"

Seba had heard many confessions in his day, but this one made him feel like he was puking and getting slapped at the same time.

All this time, those were the conditions she'd been living in? Even the first time he met her?

Suddenly, the kiss in the library and subsequent blacklisting from all of Evan Bauer's companies came into a different kind of focus.

Seba should have seen it before … and would have if he hadn't been so intent on avoiding her. But if what she was saying was true, Vic may have approached him that day the same way Seba had been approaching his target: with the intent to compromise.

That would match up with the fact that Bauer had never hired anyone to replace Seba after he'd been fired. Seba had watched for that.

It never happened.

Bauer must have gotten the information he had hired Seba for some other way—maybe through his new tech—and hadn't wanted to pay for it twice.

Seba hadn't thought it possible to hate the man more than he already did, but yep. He sure could.

Luckily, he was saved from his dark thoughts by Vic's continuing rant.

"So I'm sorry if people are sad for a few days because they think I'm dead. But the truth is that the Vic Davalos they know *needs* to die if I'm ever going to have a chance at living. Because I can't live like this anymore. I just can't!"

Seba had been expecting none of this when he broke into the hotel room.

Nothing even close.

And while he cared very much about her predicament, he couldn't let himself forget why he'd shown up.

"Okay," he said. "Let's say you're right and faking your death is the only way to get away from Bauer. I still got two letters about you regarding this weekend. How do you know someone hasn't figured out what you're up to?"

She laughed. "Someone who wants to murder me before I disappear forever on my own?" She shook her head. "How does that make any sense?"

"Maybe to make sure you don't come back?" he guessed. "Especially if you're leaving your money behind. What if they claim it and spend it, only for you to have a change of heart in a few years and reappear?"

"I'm not going to do that," she argued.

"They don't know that."

His argument seemed to resonate for a second, but then Vic shook her head. "No. No one even knows I'm doing it."

Seba held up the letters. "Someone knows. I'd say at least two people know. So unless you can name those two people and get them to verify that they sent these letters, I would suggest you get *actual* security between now and Sunday. None of the out-of-work actors you have now can do squat for you if you actually get in trouble."

That seemed to get under her skin. "Bauers men are the best!"

Seba shook his head. "I followed you last night and watched you in the club. They didn't notice me once."

She paled. "You saw me in the club?"

"From the fireball to your staggered exit," he confirmed, trying to keep his tone neutral. "Then I followed you home. They didn't notice me—or the other stalker you have."

"You followed me home." She didn't say it like a

question. She said it like, for the first time, she was scared of him.

"Don't worry," he said, keeping his tone droll. "It wasn't about you. I was testing your guys to see if they knew anything about anything. I told myself that if you were in good hands, I'd let you fend for yourself. But they missed me last night and today, just like they missed Jeff Taylor."

He watched her reaction and saw zero recognition in her eyes at the name of the owner of the fourth cloned phone. The man was following her daily and, based on the look on her face, no one had addressed it with her.

"Who?" Vic asked, happily sticking with an honest response.

"The guy in the blue shirt watching you from across the club last night," he explained. "And again from across the street when you arrived here this morning."

She had the nerve to roll her eyes at that information. "Having stalkers is written into my job description, Seba."

Even though her tone was dripping with sarcasm, something in Seba shivered when she said his name. Even said in frustration, something about how she said it sounded … right.

He brushed off the feeling. "How did he know you'd be at the club last night? How did he know you'd be here this morning?"

She shrugged. "I dunno. He probably pays paparazzi for the info. Those guys are always looking for a buck."

A plausible answer, but she shouldn't be guessing about something like that. Her people should know—especially considering what a control freak Evan Bauer was. The situation should be handled.

Nothing about anything in this conversation gelled right with what Seba already knew.

"I still don't get it," he thought aloud. "Why not tell Bauer you're done and retire? Move on to whatever you want. People would support you."

She shook her head. "If I did that, the plane crash I died in would not be fake."

Seba felt a chill of truth in her words. "You think he'd kill you?"

"Oh, I know he would," she said, sounding more angry than scared. "The only thing he cares about more than money is control and he's not going to let anyone else profit off his investment. It undermines his authority. He'd rather see me dead than answer questions on the golf course about how he lost control of me."

Several pieces slid into place in Seba's mind. He'd known more than one man like that in his life ... a lot more than one.

Her eyes dropped to the carpet. "If I quit or make Evan look bad, he will kill me and make it look like a suicide or an accident. And he'd get away with it. I'd rather disappear with a nest egg than die like that."

Based on the pinch in her voice and slight tremor in her voice, Seba believed her.

Her eyes came up again. "If he gets even the slightest whiff of what I'm planning, he'll deal with me on his own terms. So I need you to disappear back wherever you came from, okay? Everything has to look normal for the next three days. Routine. That means no new faces or narrative changes. It means I need you to leave. Now. And I need to not see you again. Ever. Do you understand?"

Yes. Seba understood.

He understood that Vic was in bigger trouble than he'd dared imagine. And she didn't even know it.

But before he could say as much, a knock came at the door, followed by a female voice from the other side. "Ms. Davalos? They're ready for you in makeup."

They'd run out of time.

Chapter 13

"You did what?" Nora gasped.

Vic had asked her manager to join her at the hotel during the lunch break, but neither woman was eating. "I know. I don't know what I was thinking."

Nora raked her hands through her hair, clearly losing all her trademark chill. "Do you know who that guy is? What he does for a living?"

Actually, no. All Vic knew was that Evan wanted her to get him fired once.

"He's a conman for hire," Nora said, some brunette strands of hair sticking between her fingers as she reached out like she wanted to shake Vic. "It's literally his job to test loyalties and get people to reveal secrets. The last time Evan hired him, he was supposed to charm his way into your step-mom's new venture and report back to Evan. Evan ended up not needing him, but this was probably Archer's second chance to impress him. And you told him *everything!*"

"Well, not everything," Vic defended. "He doesn't know where I'm going."

That earned her a groan and an eye roll. "But he knows enough to end both of us. You're not the only one risking everything on this, Vic. If Evan finds out I'm helping you—"

"He won't," Vic assured her.

"He probably already does! Your make-out buddy is probably filling him in as we speak." She checked her watch. "Evan's not due to take off for Tokyo for another six hours."

Nora's panic was contagious as it finally registered with Vic that Seba was a conman. And he'd been there to charm Miriam?

Gross.

Vic felt like puking at the thought.

The news did clear up the question of his payment amounts, however. The right secrets could go for big money. It also explained Seba's obsession with security. He was probably used to meeting *some* resistance when he took on a job, and he'd met none with her. He'd broken into her suite and she'd walked in and dumped on him like a waterfall.

Nora was right about that.

Vic had told Seba everything that mattered. If he was working for Evan, they were both screwed.

She'd messed up. Big time.

She needed to sit down. Luckily, the lounge chairs were close. Vic slumped into one of them.

"What do we do?"

Nora froze. "We? We said from the beginning that there is no 'we'. If one of us gets caught doing something, we don't bring the other into it."

Vic's stomach turned. Nora was right. They had said that. And Vic had every intention of living up to her promise.

She'd just panicked. Something about that Seba guy knocked her off center. She did crazy things when he was around … like feel lightheaded during kisses and reveal secret plots over-a-year in the making.

But after seeing Seba this morning, Vic had needed a sane person to speak to. Nora was literally the only option when it came to that, but calling her had been a mistake— *another* mistake.

She was really piling them up today.

"I shouldn't even be here," Nora said, pulling a pill bottle out of her purse. "I mean, I appreciated the heads up on your screw up, but I finished the last of my part in all of this seven months ago. I'm done. I'm out. This is all you. All I can do is act normal from here on out and hope it keeps working."

When Nora palmed a pill and popped it back without water, Vic noticed the light sheen of sweat forming on her manager.

"I'm so sorry," Vic said, standing.

"Well, sorry doesn't cut it!" Nora hissed, trading the pill bottle out for the phone in her purse and putting her finger at the ready to turn it back on. "Do you have any idea what you've done?"

"I know," Vic said as guilt washed over her. "I wasn't thinking. This guy ... he threw me for a loop—"

"You better hope that's all he did," Nora said, looking even more manic as she headed for the door. "Look, I've gotta go. I've got to get out of here. I have other things to do and so do you. What's done is done. All we can do from here on out is stick to the plan, okay?"

Vic nodded. "Okay."

Nora stopped when her hand found the door handle and shot a look back Vic's way. "Don't contact me again. No calls. No visits. We're done. I have two kids and I will not be risking them for you. Understand?"

"Totally," Vic agreed. "Again, so sorry, Nora. But ... I'm glad you know."

That got a bitter laugh out of her manager as she shook her head and jerked the door open. "Yeah. Thanks for that. Good luck."

Then she was gone—the soft-loaded spring on the door keeping it from slamming behind her.

Vic dropped back to the lounge chair, lightheaded and feeling like her stomach was twisted like a rag inside of her.

"Breathe," she told herself, counting to five on an inhale before repeating the count on an exhale. Then she repeated the process again and again until her head didn't feel so light.

"Just act normal," she whispered. "All you gotta do is what you always do. You can do this … so go do it."

Her next breath was quick. She straightened her posture on the inhale and stood on the exhale, but she faltered when it came to walking out the door with her head held high. Her eyes darted to the bed instead—to where she had stashed the phone Seba had given her.

In case you realize you need help, he'd said.

It was probably a trap or a tracking device … or both. She should have thrown it in the trash on set. Instead, she'd hid it under the mattress where she could claim a previous guest left it, if it was found.

Seba was right about one thing. Her guards weren't paid to protect her so much as report back on her. A lot of times they loosened the leash hoping she'd act out and they could report back and get bonus points.

Like this morning. Ryan might be nice but he'd almost certainly search her room while she was on set—especially now that he knew Nora had visited.

But he wouldn't lift a hotel mattress up more than a few inches, and she'd shoved it back the length of her arm after wiping her prints off it.

There was nothing tying Vic to the phone and it couldn't spy on her from under a mattress.

She'd figure out what to do with it later.

Right then, she needed to get back to work and act normal.

Nora was right. All they could do was stick to the plan.

Chapter 14

Seba counted enough chips for a raise and tossed them to the center of the poker table as the muffled audio of a hotel room door clicking shut played in his earbud.

Vic must have shoved the phone under something. Everything sounded far away, but microphones were quite advanced these days. He'd heard everything.

Part of Seba felt bad about spying on Vic, but going in blind on something this big wasn't an option.

Seba knew Evan hadn't heard his conversation with Vic that morning. He hadn't seen a phone on her, but he'd used the jammer anyway. But all that effort was for nothing if Evan had just overheard Nora and Vic's conversation like Seba had.

"I'm out," the player next to Seba said, pushing his cards to the center.

"Call," the next guy said, tossing in chips.

Seba's eyes tracked to the next man. His target.

Daddy's heir had a gambling problem and Seba was here to help scare Junior straight. But it was taking too long to get to the punch line. Whittling the rich-boy's chips down to nothing and getting him to over-bet after could take hours. And Vic didn't have hours. She needed someone watching her six right then.

After hearing the genuine terror in Nora's voice, Seba was certain Vic needed help getting to the finish line on her crazy plan. No one else was going to help, by the sounds of it. It was the eleventh hour and they were washing their hands of her.

She was going to need someone like him to succeed.

And when Saturday came, if Vic wanted to fly off into her fake death, Seba would get her safely onto that plane. It was her life. She should be able to do with it what she wanted. But Seba was now strangely invested in making sure she was alive when that plane took off.

Across from him, Junior chewed his bottom lip before deciding to call.

Seba checked his watch. 12:34. A minute later than the last time he looked.

She's fine, he told himself. *She's still on set. They're filming. She won't be done for hours.*

But the logic did nothing to keep his heart from hammering like he'd had too much caffeine.

Something was imminently wrong. He didn't know what yet, but couldn't wait until he figured it out to get into position. He had to trust his lizard brain on this one. He had to trust the difference between the tinny buzz of anxiety that moved from the lungs to the head, and the thrum of a sixth sense that moved from the gut up to the heart, making it hammer for a life-saving sprint.

Seba felt the latter on this one. The thrum .... the primal part that knew something was wrong ... that sixth sense that wouldn't shut up.

Living on the streets had taught Seba that a sixth sense was nothing more than a single sense that had picked up on something pivotal the other four hadn't clued into yet. It was a solo sense screaming in the mind for the rest of the class to catch up so they could all survive together.

And Seba's sixth sense was telling him he had to cancel

all his jobs through Sunday—right after he walked out on this one.

Doing so would be devastating to his reputation, but that seemed par for the course when it came to crossing paths with Vic Davalos.

The woman was like kryptonite.

Every time she was around, he stopped remembering everything that was important and screwed up the big stuff. He tried to blame that first time on the kiss, but the truth was she'd rewired his brain with a look and he'd forgotten why he'd shown up at the party the moment he laid eyes on her.

In the two years and three months since, Seba's work had been a model of perfection. He hadn't let a case drop once. Not one sick day or even a holiday. He never canceled or rescheduled. His word was considered by many to be gold.

Now, boom. He sees Vic again and he's back to his bad habits of ignoring what really mattered.

All because of a sixth sense that might just want to kiss her again. The gnawing sensation felt bigger than that, but all he knew was that he couldn't be sitting at a poker table playing with daddy issues when he figured it out.

Vic Davalos was all alone and she wasn't okay.

You're just imagining it, he told himself, squinting his eyes shut in hopes it might clear his jumbling thoughts a bit.

It didn't.

Instead, his mom's crime scene from so many years ago came to mind. In that long blink, he was a kid again ... standing frozen on the wrong side of yellow tape, realizing he'd been home drawing pictures of Iron Man as his mom lost the fight for her life.

When she'd needed a hero, Seba had been home drawing one.

Seba couldn't let anything like that happen again. Not after all the bedtime stories he'd told himself over the years where he imagined showing up three hours earlier to walk her home and showing up in time to save her life. All his bedtime fantasies would be a joke if Seba didn't save a woman who needed saving right under his nose.

And that meant it was time to go.

Chapter 15

The phone under the mattress was gone.

Vic had been standing, frozen—maybe not even breathing—since the realization had set in. She'd searched the bed five times, lifting the mattress every which way to find it, and found nothing.

It was definitely gone.

Vic had left it in the room somewhere after 12:30, and Ryan and Tristan had swapped out shifts around 2:30. It was now 3:45, and the phone was gone.

Either Ryan or Tristan had it. Probably Tristan. He and Bret were always in competition to impress the boss. They both wanted to be transferred to Evan's detail. It's where all the perks and prestige were. Guarding Vic was just one of the rungs on the way up. A test of loyalty, of sorts.

Now that the phone was gone, she had to assume it was because someone was looking to rise a rung on the Bauer ladder, but knew they had to wait until filming wrapped to avoid making a scene.

Avoiding public scenes was important to Evan. He valued his manicured persona very highly and part of that persona was projecting a sense of constant control and composure. He moved like flowing lava in public, and saved the eruptions

108

for closed doors.

Evan's ability to compartmentalize had made it impossible for Vic to ask for help over the years. When she reached out, she always became the crazy, irrational one spouting crazy stories while Evan stayed calm and proper— assuring people he'd handle Vic when she was calmed down enough to be rational again.

Everyone was always so relieved when Vic was back to being "herself" in his capable hands ... hands she'd steered clear of for a while now but, with this phone incident, she might have reached the end of her run.

She'd know for sure once the scene wrapped. The film's leads were scheduled to move to a sunset location at 4:30. That meant Vic had forty-five minutes, at best, before the director let her go.

Then she would see if Tristan took her home or if he took her somewhere else.

If he took her somewhere else, it was her own fault.

She'd screwed up twice in one day and tipped her hand. There was no one to blame but herself. Either Ryan had checked her room after Nora made her unscheduled visit, or Tristan had searched it when he came on shift.

Or ... maybe Nora was right and Seba had been hired to expose her. If so, her fate had been sealed the moment she'd spilled to him, instead of kicking him out of her room and calling security.

Whatever the case, she'd deviated from a plan that had worked for over a year and—three days from freedom— she'd been caught.

Evan would be furious.

But Vic couldn't think about that now. She had to finish filming like everything was normal ... like she didn't know anything about any phone ... like it was a normal day. Anything that didn't look normal made her look crazy and there were too many cameras around for her to freak out.

She'd made that mistake too many times before.

She had to stay calm ... normal ... totally calm and normal.

"Breathe," she told herself, forcing an inhale.

When a knock came at the door, Vic jumped.

"Yes?" she answered in reflex and her voice sounded like it usually did. That was good.

"Ms. Davalos?" a male voice said through the door. "We tweeted a meet-and-greet for fans down on the sidewalk. You're invited to change out of your costume and join the cast for pictures and autographs."

Vic started sweating at the realization that they were wrapping the location. A cold sweat sheened over her as she stood frozen where she was, mouth-breathing and heart pounding.

She needed to answer the guy. That was the normal thing to do.

"Sounds good," she called out, still looking at the bed. "I'll be right down."

Tristan was right outside the door so he'd heard her answer. The ball was in his court now as to whether he was going to make a scene to get her to Evan before he left for the airport.

That was her one hope in all of this.

Evan's scheduled take-off was at six, and her step-father prided himself on his punctuality. He'd probably head to the airport around 5:00.

If Vic could burn the next hour, maybe he would put off dealing with her until he got back.

And she'd be gone by then.

Vic changed back into what she had arrived in that morning—leggings and an oversized tee no one was paying her to wear. Now that pictures would be involved, Evan would be mad about that, too.

Man. She was really racking up the points.

"You have a gig at nine," she reminded herself when thoughts of punishment came to mind.

Evan knew about the gig. Plus, she had at least eight meetings the next day.

Evan knew that, too.

Tipping her chin up, Vic walked out of the room to find Tristan facing her, hands clasped behind his back.

"You should have declined," he said.

Normal. "I have time. I'm free until nine."

His eyes narrowed, clearly scanning her for signs of guilt.

"Don't worry," she snarked. "The video games will still be there when we get home."

Oh, that got him. His jaw clenched, his nostrils flared, and his chin tilted down dangerously.

He knew about the phone. For sure.

Somehow Vic pulled up the gumption to scoff at his reaction. "Please. Don't pretend that's not exactly what you do while you're waiting for me."

When he said nothing, Vic headed for the elevator and he fell in step behind her. She opened Instagram for the silent ride to the lobby level, pretending she didn't notice Tristan's vibe was dark as tar. She just scrolled, forcing normal breathing, as she pressed the hearts under pictures she passed to change them red.

What felt like an eternity later, the elevator gently jerked to a stop and dinged a beat before the doors parted, revealing one of the PAs waiting for her.

"Hey, Vic," she said with a bright smile. "Great scene today."

"Thanks, Zara," Vic said, returning the smile. "Where we headed?"

"To the side of the building, away from the entrance," Zara said, handing her two Sharpies. "Follow me."

"Cool," Vic said, just to say something. Or maybe because Tristan's gaze was like a cold chill from behind as she followed Zara down a hall that led to a side exit.

"There's a decent group," Zara said, trying to sound like she cared. "More will probably show, but don't feel obligated to stay too long."

"Sure," Vic said as Tristan pulled out his phone and texted something.

Then they were outside the door, stepping into a makeshift pen surrounded by maybe fifty people angling for autographs.

"That's Vic Davalos!" a nearby girl hissed to her friend before yelling, "Vic, can I get a selfie?"

Leaving Tristan to stand against the wall of the building, Vic headed over to the friends and took pictures with them before pulling the cap off her first Sharpie and signing whatever people thrust her way. Hats. Shirts. A signature book. Someone even handed her a street flyer.

"Omigosh! I love you!"

"Thank you," Vic said, taking the flyer. "Who should I sign this to?"

"Mary," she said beaming. "Spelled the usual way."

Vic started signing. "Where are you from, Mary?"

The girl blushed. "Oh, my gosh. You can totally tell I'm not from here. I'm acting like a loser, aren't I?"

Vic smiled, handing the flyer back. "Not at all—"

"Missouri," the girl answered, recovering in record time. "We're here on vacation. The rest of my family is eating down the street but I saw the tweet and knew I had to come."

"Well, good to meet you, Mary from Missouri."

The girl blushed. "Omigosh. You gave me a nickname. I'm dying. I'm literally dying right now."

Vic smiled at the girl's excitement. It was almost enough to make her forget Tristan looming as she moved on from Mary to the next person and the next.

Maybe her autograph might actually be worth something after she disappeared. She might be handing people money in the bank.

The crowd grew—some people starting to show up with actual pictures of her or magazines she'd been on the cover of—items getting thrust in front of her faster than she could sign them.

Vic was getting into the groove when a black SUV caught her eye across the street.

Her SUV.

But Tristan was standing behind her, which meant someone else was driving.

"Can you sign this to Tyler?" someone asked as both Bret and Ryan stepped out of the vehicle across the street. "It's for his birthday."

No Chloe on the scene. Just the guys.

Chloe was Evan's unofficial witness to how paranoid Vic was. So if the men were leaving Chloe out of whatever came next, they weren't going anywhere with witnesses.

"Sure," Vic said, taking the picture and totally blanking on what she was supposed to do with it. "How do you spell the name?"

The woman looked at her like she was an idiot. "T-Y-L-E-R. The usual way."

"Right," Vic beamed, the original request returning to mind. "Just don't want to mess up his name for his birthday."

The girl's critical look faded. "Right. Thanks."

"Sure," Vic said, doing her best not to look past the crowd to the car across the street as she looked down and spelled 'Tyler' wrong. She gave it two 'e's for some reason and there was no way to fix it. And her hand was sweating.

"Are you okay?" the girl asked.

Inhaling in reflex, Vic looked up with a practiced smile. "Oh, yeah. I just feel dumb. I totally spelled his name wrong."

To her surprise, the girl laughed. "That's what you get for being careful. That's when I always screw up."

"Right," Vic said, doing her best to fix it before adding her signature under the botch.

Ryan and Bret weren't crossing the street. They stayed where they were … waiting.

"Thank you," the girl said.

"Hope it's a great birthday," Vic said with her best version of a smile.

They were trying to freak her out and she couldn't let them. They either wanted to pressure her into cutting out early or panic her into creating a scene that could be spun into a headline about her instability.

She wouldn't give it to them.

If they wanted to get her to Evan before he left for the airport, it was their move.

"Hi," she said to the next face, not asking about a name this time.

She signed on auto-pilot—hand still slippery and starting to cramp. Three signatures later, Vic was messing up her own name and she could feel her heart racing in her throat.

She was starting to lose it. She knew the feeling well, and could already feel the edges of vertigo creeping in. All of a sudden, everyone felt too close—their voices too loud and expressions larger than life … like they all knew she was faking and they were faking with her.

Stop it, stop it, stop it, she told herself. *You're making it easy. If you have a breakdown, that's it. Game over. So pull it together!*

And while her soul was willing, her body was crumbling.

"I don't have anything to sign," said the next person. "Can we take a selfie?"

"Sure." Big smile. Click.

"Thanks."

"You're welcome."

Breathe. And next.

She hadn't used that mantra for a while, but it was what she needed.

Everything's normal, she told herself as she fumbled her name on the next picture. *Totally normal.*

Only it wasn't. The moment she left the protection of this crowd, normal might not be normal ever again. There would be new rules … new punishments … and there was nothing she could do about it.

She could go full-Britney in this moment—shave her head and chase her team with an umbrella—and no one would think her sane until she started performing again.

And it was while imagining shaved heads and umbrellas that Vic realized she'd gone too far this time.

Seba had been right that morning: faking her death was way too big—such a betrayal to all the fans who would help her if they could.

But they couldn't.

Because if they tried, her step-father would squash them to the point of making sure they were incapable of helping anyone ever again. And Vic couldn't do that to a fan—beg for help here and now and get someone to destroy their lives without really knowing what they were signing up for. It wouldn't be fair to a fan.

It wouldn't even be fair to do that to an enemy.

That's why Vic had told herself it was better to remove herself from the equation—let someone who actually wanted the job take it, then let everyone move on and forget about her.

People's attention spans were short and money was greased lightning in Hollywood. Everyone would move on and Vic would have a life. In Iceland.

She still remembered the feeling of walking down a street when she'd been there for a shoot the year before. Days had been short and nights long, with the Aurora Borealis lighting up the sky. And no matter where Vic went, no one had a clue who she was.

She hadn't wanted to leave.

Fast-forward a year later and she had a plane ready to dump in the ocean to convince the world she was dead. All while leaving her family legacy and wealth in Evan's hands.

What had she been thinking?

Maybe Evan was right. Maybe she really was crazy.

She didn't know anymore. All she knew was that it was

time to stop stalling and find out what Evan knew and what he planned on doing about it. Making him late for his flight was not only petty, it would make the punishment worse.

Might as well just face the music.

The moment Vic made the decision, resignation washed over her and she looked over the crowd with a sense of sadness.

She might not be seeing people like this for a while, but it was what it was.

"That's it for me," she said, giving the group a wave as she stepped away from the barriers. "Thanks for stopping by."

And she meant it. Some people in the crowd might be jerks but there were a few in there that would save her if they could—like Mary from Missouri. She would try to help. Vic was sure of it.

But Vic couldn't even help herself. All she could do was go where her guards took her. Because that was her life.

Turning to face Tristan, she gave him a totally normal nod. "Let's go."

Chapter 16

Tracking Vic's team from the hotel, the last place Seba expected to end up was another hotel. This one was smaller and fully off of Seba's radar. He thought he'd worked everywhere in the city, but this location had eluded him.

Probably not an accident.

Yelp had listed it as "boutique" and pricey.

Seba watched as the SUV skipped the valet service, choosing to drive to the underground parking on their own. He had to assume that they didn't want the staff seeing Vic arrive.

Seba didn't like it.

Nor did he like the idea of sitting outside waiting for something to happen. Because something big was about to. He could feel it in his bones. People only went to local hotels when they wanted to hide or keep the aftermath of something away from their home.

Whatever the case, things were about to get tricky. Seba was blacklisted in the Bauer camp, and Vic had recognized him that morning without so much as a blink of hesitation. One glance, and she had gone full deer in headlights.

Seba had to assume that anyone in the Bauer camp would recognize him just as quickly. So no showing his face in

117

person or appearing on hotel security footage.

Getting in would be easy, but if he wanted to get out with Vic, he needed an exit strategy.

He flipped through options in his head—dismissing most out of the gate and waiting until he found one that resonated like the warm sense of victory.

Pulling up DHack's business number, he gave it a call.

"What do you need?" came DHack's signature greeting.

"Got two drivers who want to make a grand tonight?"

Chapter 17

It had been a while since Vic had been in this room, with its soundproof walls and discreet staff. But rather than panicking, a strange sort of calm washed over her at the predictability of what came next.

The jaded parts of her almost found it humorous.

The current vibe was *so* twelve years ago. It reminded her of her first days in the Bauer household, surrounded by staff instructed not to acknowledge her or grant any requests. They were to act like she wasn't there—occasionally speaking about her in generic pronouns, but never speaking to her.

Vic had to admit that the tactic had been effective on the younger version of her. She'd still been reeling from her parents' death and she'd gone straight from that trauma to a home where everyone had treated her like she was invisible. She'd felt like a ghost ... like maybe she'd died, too, and was the last to know it.

Older Vic knew better. It was one of Evan's many mind games that tested people on all sides—rewarding his in-group while leaving everyone else in uncertain territory. Knowing where one stood with Evan was easy. Insiders had names and outsiders were referred to in generic terms, reinforcing the idea that they were interchangeable and disposable.

Surviving Evan Bauer meant paying attention and being smarter the next time around while always reading the signs. So that's what Vic did as she pretended to casually scroll through Instagram.

But her eyes were on the room, not the screen.

Her own guards were acting like she wasn't there which meant stakes were high. The four guards in Evan's travel team were present, which meant he hadn't left for the airport yet.

Vic told herself that wasn't a big deal until the clock on her phone read 5:15. The window for Evan to take off on time for Tokyo was closing. Fast. And that was bad for her.

"What are we waiting for?" she asked everyone in the room. "You realize I have an appearance to make tonight, right?"

No answer.

Vic hadn't expected one, but two could play when it came to Evan's mind games. Sometimes how someone *didn't* answer communicated a lot more than how they did. Sometimes it was tension revealing their discomfort; sometimes it was shared glances, revealing alliances; sometimes it was the choice of what someone pretended to find interesting.

Vic hadn't made it as far as she had in life by not being able to read a room.

Evan's travel team was casually in position around her, eyes on their phones and seeming to occasionally share images or screenshots with each other. On the surface, they were chilling, but they were also one perk-up away from looking official.

Next to the door, Tristan and Bret looked like they were competing for best of show. Vic had actually never seen them look so official in all of her time with them.

They were definitely looking to impress.

Ryan was in the other room, keeping himself out of sight. He was the weak link in all this, but he'd go with the group when push came to shove. He'd just question his life choices and have a restless night's sleep before clocking back in tomorrow. Guys like him always came back with some sort of story about how if he didn't do it, someone else would, and they might not be as nice about it. So it might as well be him.

Because ... nicer.

But weak links were weak links. Evan had taught Vic that over the years. When it came to being either the hero or the villain, their hearts failed. They didn't have it in them to rise to either occasion.

So, if tonight was a test, Ryan was on his way out and Tristan and Bret were ready to impress while aiming for upward momentum.

Vic also knew what to expect from Evan's personal team. They were as cold as steel. Like he'd trained them to be. Anything that came from them tonight would be cold and efficient. It was her own team she had to watch out for.

She kept scrolling.

5:19 p.m., and no Evan. Things were not looking good.

Her phone buzzed.

Oh, she got a new follower on Instagram. And a comment!

SICK!!! I need this in my life! it read, followed by heart-eyes and fire emojis.

Smiling despite everything, Vic clicked to see which picture the commenter was talking about and grinned when the shot of the first suit she ever made popped up.

Thank you! Vic typed, replying to the comment. *And thanks for the follow. It gives me life!*

Vic's phone buzzed with another like. Then another. The other person seemed to be going through her profile and liking pretty much everything.

Someone after Vic's own heart. And she must have shared Vic's profile, too, because more likes and followers started making her phone buzz non-stop.

If everything else in her world was about to go wrong, at least this one thing was going right. People were finally finding her work and they liked what they saw.

Maybe there was hope.

Vic was so distracted, she didn't look at the time again until 6:04. Then she went from elated to ill in a heartbeat.

Evan should be in the air and his travel team was in a room with her.

He'd postponed his trip. And, given the people in the room with her, there was a 100% chance she was the cause.

Breathe, she told herself, trying to get excited about Instagram again, but it was useless. The stakes around her had just been raised to an unprecedented level. Not once, in all the time Vic had known Evan, had he changed his plans on account of her.

Not ever.

The sun was dropping on the horizon—not setting yet, but getting there. Off somewhere, the people she'd been working with all day were probably filming a scene. Others were leaving work and going home for dinner. Maybe they'd watch whatever was on TV Thursday nights or maybe they'd go out.

Vic stared off at nothing and pretended she was each one of them as the sun faded and the sky turned dark.

7:11.

There was nothing to do but wait now.

Chapter 18

The wait was killing Seba.

Vic was in the building. He knew it—he felt it—but all the rooms were surprisingly quiet. He was monitoring ambient sound and vibrations on each of the hotel's seven levels and wasn't getting any hits.

Most guests were probably out for dinner or doing other things out-of-towners did.

Finding Vic should have been easy, but this hotel had a few security features that definitely didn't come standard.

Boutique, indeed.

Seba hadn't packed the equipment he needed to make walls disappear and see what lay beyond. He was using his one camera to keep eyes on the SUV in underground parking and using mics on the hotel itself, and that was about the best he could do.

But it wasn't enough. He was coming up on three hours without contact and anything could be happening.

"Wait, what's this?" he asked the room as a second SUV pulled into view on the garage cam and parked next to the first.

The vehicles were identical.

Seba leaned in, tense as he waited to see who got out. He almost cheered a sigh of relief when two guards exited and one of them opened the door for none other than Evan Bauer, who got out with a phone pressed to his ear.

Seba was in the right spot. Vic was in the building and, if Evan was just getting there, she was some version of okay.

He'd want to talk to her.

The three men headed straight for the elevator and Seba was trying to read the man's lips as he spoke on the phone when the two-way radio in his bag started broadcasting.

"...*send the pilot a gift of our appreciation,*" Bauer was saying, three pairs of heavy footsteps echoing off concrete in the background. There was also a swishing sound of fabric, making it sound like the phone he'd given Vic that morning was in a pocket.

Who had turned it on? And why?

Was it a trap?

Trap or not, Seba kept listening in. And watching.

On the camera, Bauer hung up without another word. On the radio, footsteps continued about twenty more paces until the first pair of shoes stopped. There was the soft click of an elevator button being punched, immediately followed by a ding of readiness by the elevator before the doors parted.

The moment they stepped inside, Seba lost visual and went for his backpack, digging the phone out and holding it close to his ear.

"*If we move to Plan B, keep who you want to keep,*" Bauer said through the speaker. "*Have them handle the others.*"

"*Yes, sir,*" the man closest to the mic replied.

They made the rest of the ride in silence, the ping of arrival sounding through the phone a beat before it registered on his seventh-floor microphone.

Of course, they were in the penthouse.

The question was how could Seba get in there, and how many men would he find when he got there?

He needed a plan.

Chapter 19

Vic knew the moment her step-father arrived at the location because all the men came to attention.

Those who were lounging quit lounging.

Tristan and Bret stood up even straighter.

Ryan re-entered the main room.

8:23 p.m.

She'd been sitting in the same chair for over three hours.

A few minutes after everyone perked up, the main door opened and Evan walked in with his two most-trusted, Hawkins and Ellis.

Evan made a show of greeting all the men first, like he had all the time in the world and she was the least interesting thing in the room. He thought it was a power play—and maybe it was for most people—but it had stopped working on Vic when she'd been somewhere around sixteen.

Pretending to ignore the one reason everyone was in a room just made Evan look small in Vic's eyes. And she had no interest in bending to the will of such a small man. If he wanted to pretend she was below his notice and inconsequential, that's what Vic would give him when he was done preening for his men.

When his jacket came off, Vic didn't give Evan the

pleasure of a reaction. And when he rolled his sleeves up, she swore to spit on his shirt if he made her bleed.

But she doubted he would. She had a lot of appointments tomorrow.

When he finally looked her way, his expression was deceptively calm. "Game's up, kitten. You have some explaining to do."

She furrowed her brow. "No one told me why I'm here. All I know is that I'm definitely going to be late to my next appointment."

Evan shook his head as he stood over her. "Wrong answer."

"Well, I don't even know what you're asking," she countered. "So you're going to have to let me in on what game you think you're playing right now."

That was also a wrong answer. She knew it before the words left her mouth but let them rip anyway.

Too much attitude. Too impertinent. But rather than growing angry, he looked amused as he held out his hand to the side. Hawkins reached into his jacket and pulled out the phone from that morning. Seba's phone.

Once it was in Evan's hand, he held it out between them. "Let's start with this."

Vic looked from the phone to him and shrugged. "It's not mine."

His jaw tensed in annoyance. "Don't play dumb. It was found in your hotel room after Nora's visit."

"Then it was there before her visit," Vic countered, sticking to the truth. "She was there to talk about maybe pairing me up again."

Those had been Nora's first words when she stepped through the hotel room door earlier so hopefully she'd stuck to them and they were telling the same story.

Evan motioned for a chair and Ellis slid one into place like a true gentleman. But Evan sat like no lady as he leaned forward in the seat and held the phone out as if offering it to

126

her.

Vic didn't touch it.

"Where did the phone come from?" he asked.

"It must have been in the room before I got there."

Also, true. Vic had always found it was best to stick to the truth when lying. Seba had been in the room before her, thus, the phone had been, too.

Evan shook his head like he pitied her. "Then why wasn't it found during the initial sweep?"

"Uh, maybe because there wasn't one," she said, leaning into the impatience she imagined any innocent person would feel. "And I wasn't even in the room, really, until Nora came to talk about options. We got there, like, ten minutes before I went to makeup and were filming on the rooftop. I pretty much stayed by the pool all day."

"Sounds like a hard day at work," he mocked.

"I do as I'm told," Vic replied, letting some of her contempt slide through. He didn't miss it.

"What about the plane you bought nine months ago? Know anything about that?"

She felt herself blink wrong in answer. A quick blink and inhale of a guilty person, not the stalled breath and confused gaze of someone hearing something for the first time.

She had to go with it.

"Fine. I have a plane. I might want to learn how to fly it, too. Is that a sin?"

Yes. It was. But it was a lesser sin than the truth.

He leaned back, assessing her. "So you admit to the plane but not to the phone?"

"It's not my phone," she said, holding up the one in her hand and giving it a jiggle. "Mine's right here."

Evan held the phone up next to his shoulder and Hawkins put it back into his pocket. With his hands empty, Evan threaded his fingers together in front of him—his top thumb drumming out an even beat on the other.

"The problem with you," he said after a few beats, "is

that you're getting good. You have a gift of turning inches into miles, and that has me sitting here wondering if you're even worth the effort anymore."

Worth the effort? Vic forced herself not to react.

He gestured out toward the room. "I surround you with nice things and give you a life other girls dream of, and all you ever do is pay me back with spite and slander."

Still, she couldn't help but respond. "Maybe because it's not my dream. Maybe because I didn't ask for *any* of this."

He laughed, angling back to the guys as he said, "Listen to this part, men. This is the soliloquy of every spoiled woman. Give her everything and she'll make up something you missed and blame you for it."

This time Vic leaned forward, too angry to hold back. "Oh, I don't blame you for anything you missed. I blame you for what you did." She started counting them on her fingers. "I blame you for selling pictures of me to the paparazzi when I was fourteen—"

"Which started your modeling career," he countered.

"I blame you for getting my parents addicted to heroin and keeping them supplied with enough to kill an elephant."

"They made their choices," he said through his teeth. "You think I wanted them dead? They were hit-making machines. You have no idea how much I lost when they died."

How much *he* lost?

In a flash, Vic remembered who she was talking to and how useless it was to talk back. It was a one-way path to appearing hysterical to anyone who walked in on the conversation half-way through. Especially when the sorrow of losing her parents hit and she started crying.

Yeah, she wouldn't be giving Evan that. Not tonight.

Tonight, she would accept her punishment with her signature look then see if she could find some blogger who wanted to risk it all at the next party she made it to. It was time to end this madness.

But that wouldn't be happening be tonight. She was coming to terms with that.

Seeming to make a decision, Evan stood and started rolling down his sleeves.

That was ... unexpected.

"You know," he mused. "When you came into my home, I had no idea what a headache I was signing up for."

"Only that you'd been embezzling from my parents and had to make it look right somehow?" she snapped.

"No," he said, holding his hand out for a cufflink that Ellis made appear. "I thought you might be worth something. Turns out I was wrong."

He intended the words to break her. Vic could see it in his eyes. But, for some reason, she found the accusation hilarious.

"You wish I was worthless," she laughed. "You're just mad I'm not a puppet like your lap dogs here."

"No," he said, doing up his first cufflink. "You're not. Everyone here is playing their part but you. You're the only one who thinks she should have to play by a different set of rules while never thanking me for protecting you all these years."

"Protecting me?" she scoffed. "From what?"

He reached out for the second cufflink. "From me."

The humor disappeared from the situation in a cold snap.

He slid the second cufflink in place. "When you first came into our home, it was agreed that Miriam would handle you. Turns out, she wasn't up for the challenge. I had to step in back then just like I do now." Cuff affixed, he brushed invisible lint off of his sleeves. "Miriam says she's doing something to handle you, but I can't leave the country wondering what you're up to with all of us gone."

Vic's heart froze as he sent her a stern look that was laced with something more.

"You'll deny it, but we both know you plan on flying off to Iceland this weekend to chase some fantasy. And even if that phone in the hotel wasn't yours, it did me a service. I've spent the past three hours figuring out what you're up to, and I don't have three more to waste. So we're going to handle this now."

Run.

Every instinct Vic had was screaming the same thing, but with ten unfriendly men between her and the door, she didn't have a shot.

Scream!

No! It'll only encourage them. Be rational!

"Look, I'm not going anywhere this weekend," she said. "If you don't believe me, just leave two of your guys to watch me to make sure."

"You're not worth it," Evan said. "All you want to do is take everything I've given you and run off somewhere and rebrand yourself a self-made woman. Which you definitely are not. So when that whole quest fails, you'll go running back to what you do know and try to sell yourself to my competition. And we both know I don't have a reputation for letting other men profit off things I've built."

"You did not *build* me!"

Looking dismayed, Evan shook his head and motioned for his jacket.

"Unthankful to the end," he said, sending an all-business nod to Hawkins.

Hawkins, in turn, looked the direction of Bret and Tristan. "You're up."

Their chins came up in readiness.

"Toss her out the window," Hawkins said, as Evan shrugged into his jacket and started for the door.

Everything in Vic froze, not knowing where to go or what to do. In her stunned moment of panic, she noticed that Tristan and Bret had the grace to at least look surprised by the command.

Bret recovered first, crossing the room with surprising speed. It was then Vic realized she'd been seated in a corner for a reason. There was nowhere to go.

She tried for a hit when Bret got close, knowing it was futile before he proved it by catching her arm with ease and whipping her around. She rammed into someone who grabbed her from behind.

Probably Tristan.

She kicked back against his legs, earning a grunt before arms clamped around her thighs and her feet lifted off the ground.

She was pretty sure she was screaming as she kicked and pushed, yet somehow Evan's casual stroll to the door caught her eye. The travel team encircled him while Hawkins and Ellis had their eyes on her situation—making sure Bret and Tristan followed through.

Vic was doing her best to kick free when she heard Evan say, "They say sometimes you survive a fall from this height. In a way, I hope you do."

Then he was out the door, and Ellis walked over to the largest penthouse window that cracked open at an angle.

"If she doesn't fit out this, we can take her to the roof," he said and Tristan and Bret seemed eager to have the job done. They moved quickly, absorbing her struggles with frustrating ease.

Everything started to blur from there. People spoke, their voices calm and instructive. But Vic's mind didn't really hear what they said, only that the latch used to close the window stabbed into her ribs and that when she flinched away from the pain, she felt the hands under her shoulders release. Then the street came into view.

The building was smooth. Nothing to hold on to. The sound of wind filled her ears, paired with the sounds of light traffic.

Below her, street lights glowed and cars drove, and everything looked normal. Totally normal.

"She fits!"

Then the grip around her legs released and Vic's stomach

lurched as she started to drop.

Chapter 20

Seba was in position on the roof when he heard the scream.

Vic's scream.

"No," he gasped, running for the ledge while bracing himself for the sound of an impact as he cursed himself.

The windows in his room had been bolted shut. How was he supposed to know the penthouse was different? He'd thought they'd have to take Vic to the roof so that's where he'd gone.

But, apparently, the penthouse had windows that opened. And Vic fit. And he heard her scream, but nothing since.

He couldn't look, but he had to. If she was dead, it was his fault in more ways than one.

Certain he was about to be sick, he moved to the ledge.

Just then, his phone buzzed with a text. The interruption kicked him out of the moment and he opened it in reflex.

Room 606.

That's all it said.

Room 606 ... what?

Feeling more lost than ever, Seba looked off the edge of the roof to the sidewalk below and saw ... pedestrians walking normally ... no cars stopping ... no body.

He looked back at his phone.

Room 606.

Seba started running.

Chapter 21

One moment, Vic was free falling with only a street below her, and the next she was bouncing sideways across carpet—sharp bites marking each contact with the rug until she skidded to a stop at the foot of a bed.

Instead of a glowing street, she saw a hotel ceiling.

Her stomach twisted like she still believed it was falling and when she grimaced against the sick feeling, her mind saw the street again.

She forced her eyes open, looking at the ceiling again. Then the wall. Then some framed image of a sunset that screamed 'hotel'.

Vic really was back in the hotel. She had no idea how, but she was.

The lights were on in the room and she used the light to check herself for damage on instinct. A few rug burns on her elbow and the outside of her arm from the carpet but, otherwise, she was remarkably intact.

Her eyes moved to the inside of her forearm of their own accord, her other hand coming up to gently touch the skin there. Somewhere in the back of her mind, there seemed to be the memory of a sense of being grabbed like a trapeze artist ... but only by one arm ... the slap of a palm on her forearm

… a yank on her shoulder before she started moving a new direction.

Vic turned her arm over, looking for marks, but the only redness she saw could have been from the carpet. She closed her eyes, trying to remember what had happened, and suddenly her mind was falling again.

She opened her eyes, gasping, and crab walked across the room until her back hit a wall. She pressed into it, pushing her feet into the carpet to make the feeling go away.

She hadn't fallen.

She *should* have fallen. But for some impossible reason she hadn't.

She hadn't.

She was alive.

She was alive in a hotel and nothing made sense.

Then the door popped open on the other side of the wall and Vic's heart stopped when it clicked shut.

"Vic?" someone whisper-yelled and Vic could have sworn she knew the voice.

Still, she hid, scrunching herself into the smallest ball she could while praying whoever it was would move on and not search too hard.

She knew she hadn't gotten her wish when footsteps moved her way and the draft she hadn't noticed yet faded.

Whoever was in the room was close enough to block the A/C vent, or something like it.

Fight like you mean it this time, she thought before looking up and finding … nothing. Just the ceiling.

Then she looked over toward where the door was and saw the last person she expected. His frame was distinct, even from behind, as he stood in front of the window and stretched his hand through where the pane should be.

She was clearly imagining things. There was no reason for Seba to be there. It wasn't like she'd kicked him out nicely that morning. She'd basically called him useless and shown him the door.

He couldn't be here. She had to be seeing things.

Maybe she really was dead and this was just her not believing it.

As if sensing her gaze, Seba turned from the window and looked straight at her.

"Vic," he breathed, rushing up to her. "How did you manage this?"

He was asking *her*? Vic hadn't done a thing. Literally, nothing. She'd barely even fought for her life. She doubted if she left a single bruise on either of the men who had dumped her like garbage.

"Vic?"

Why hadn't she fought harder? It was like her brain had forgotten everything she'd ever learned and just panicked. Adrenaline was supposed to make people stronger, but she'd just felt less coordinated and weaker.

She still did.

"Vic?" Seba said, framing her face with his giant hands. "I need you to look up into my eyes, Vic, so I can see if you're hearing me."

It took a moment to realize she wasn't looking at him, just thinking about him. But part of her was afraid that if she really looked at him, he would disappear.

But she looked up anyway.

"Hey, there," he said gently when their eyes met. The perma-smolder was gone. He looked worried.

"I think you're in shock, Vic," he said, his deep voice soft.

She wanted to say she was fine, but her body wouldn't cooperate with anything she was currently thinking.

"I didn't see what happened," he said. "But what you just experienced, it was a lot, right?"

She nodded, seeing the street in her mind and trying to blink it away. But that only made her see it more.

"Whatever just happened was way more than you can take in right now, and that's why you're in shock," he said gently. "Your senses haven't pieced it all together yet. That's something you'll figure out later, after you know you're safe. But right now we're in danger and we have to go. Do you understand me?"

He waited for an answer, and Vic wanted to say that she knew they were in trouble, but she didn't want it to be true. She just wanted to stay here with him and just have everything be okay.

"I know you're in shock and what I'm about to ask is unfair, but I need you to decide—right now—if you trust me. Because, if you do, I need to get you out of here while it's still an option." He pushed some hair away from her face. "Do you trust me to keep you safe, Vic?"

Suddenly, she found her voice again.

"Yes, you," she breathed. "If you're really here, I'm with you."

"Okay." His tone was soft. Calm. Reassuring. "Do you know if you have your phone on you?"

Her phone? No. Her phone was gone. It had been in her hand and now it wasn't. It was gone.

She shook her head. "No. I dropped it, I think."

"Good," he said. "That's good because it lets them track you. So you did good by dropping it, okay? That was a good thing."

He said it like praise, even though dropping it was nothing more than an accident.

Still, it felt good to maybe have something going right.

"Let's start with standing up," he said next, rising himself and holding his hand out to help her up. When his hand clasped around hers, she felt the phantom clasp of another hand on her forearm and sensed that the last hand to grab her had been much smaller.

"Perfect," Seba said when she was on her feet. "From here on out, keep your eyes on my feet, okay? They'll tell you where to go, when to turn, and when to stop. You don't need to look anywhere else. You just need to do what they do, okay?"

Vic nodded, part of her screaming she wasn't a child but the rest of her happy to know one thing for sure in that moment.

If she just did what his feet did, everything would be fine. She could do that.

"Okay," she said.

Chapter 22

Vic's grip was like a vice on his hand, but Seba had no complaints. She kept a great pace as they raced down the stairs to the parking garage.

He shouldn't have parked there. When he'd made the decision, he'd been thinking about the acoustics and the useless guards Vic usually had.

He could take those guys no problem. But Bauer's top brass?

All Seba could do was pray they were still up in the penthouse waiting for the other guys to report back. There had been at least four men left in the room after Bauer left, but those were the only ones Seba had heard talking.

There might be more.

"Two more flights to go," he coached before bringing his phone up to his mouth with his other hand and saying, "Positions. It's on."

"Who are you talking to?" she asked.

"Allies," he said, giving her vice grip a reassuring squeeze. "Just keep coming. We're almost there. How do you feel about motorcycles?"

"Motorcycles?" she echoed.

"Yeah. It's what I brought tonight," he said, hoping to

140

soothe her with casual talk. "You okay with that?"

Her feet faltered before finding a rhythm again. "I'm not allowed on motorcycles."

"Throw the rule book out the window," he said, guiding her around the next turn. "Do you want to ride on one?"

"Y-yeah."

"Perfect. Because that's where we're headed next," he coached. "One more flight and we're there."

"Okay."

She was doing better than he'd hoped when he first saw her staring at him like a ghost. She'd been so pale. And when her hand took his, it had been freezing cold. Yet she'd gotten up and started running when he asked.

Most people would have crumbled.

Seba didn't know her very well yet, but whoever Vic Davalos was, she had grit. He respected that.

When they reached the last step, he slowed his pace and she followed suit without a word.

"Stand behind me while I see if the coast is clear, okay?"

"Okay," she said, falling behind him but seeming unwilling to let go of his hand. He worked with the grip, cracking the door open to see what he could see.

He spotted nothing out of the ordinary, but when the door creaked a pair of shoes scuffed to a stop and froze. No talking. No second pair of shoes. It was very likely there was only one guard.

"Vic?" he whispered. "There's someone out there and I can't leave you in here while I take care of him."

"Where do you need me?" she whispered back.

He nearly breathed a sigh of relief at her comprehension of the situation. "I need you to go left and around the corner when we walk out this door. I'll go right and fight, then come get you okay?"

Her grip tightened somehow.

"You ready to let go of my hand?" he asked.

"Oh. Yeah," she breathed. A second later, the circulation

141

returned to his hand.

"What do you do when I open this door?"

"Left, around the corner, hide until you come get me," she replied.

"Yes," he said as the feet in the garage started moving again.

Seba pulled the door open, walking through and stretching into his full height as Vic blissfully followed instructions and disappeared around the corner behind him.

Smoothie guard from that morning was on his way over to check out the door, but his steps slowed when he saw who he was up against. The man visibly faltered while they were still a good ten feet apart.

"It's not too late to do the right thing," Seba said. "Let us go."

Uncertainty morphed into conviction as the man brought a comm up to his lips. "They're in the garage."

Seba swore under his breath, covering the distance between them to bat away the man's attack and knock him out. The guy fell like a tree—cheek hitting the concrete first and Seba couldn't help but feel a rush of satisfaction.

Man, that felt good. His only regret was that he couldn't do it again.

He was just about to turn back Vic's direction and lead her to the bike when he heard racing steps from the main parking entrance. Two pairs of shoes. And they were coming in fast.

Seba readied himself, knowing he could take two of these clowns at the same time.

Then the elevator dinged.

Great. Since when were elevators so fast?

A few seconds later, four men were in full view and incoming.

This was bad. At least two of these guys were the real deal. They were trained for maximum damage and their master had just taken them off-leash.

One-against-one would be an even fight.

Two-against-one would be Seba showing off.

Three-against-one would be making sure he made everyone bleed before letting fate pick the winner.

But four-against-one? There was little chance of losing with any amount of dignity against those odds. Yet giving up wasn't an option. He'd promised to get Vic to safety and a man was only as good as his word, so this fight was on.

Four-against-one.

Bring it—

Wait. Another guard was running down the ramp so make that five-against-on—

No. Make that six.

Six-against-one.

Every choice leading up to this moment was going to haunt Seba later. He knew it. He'd been an idiot to park in the garage. That was clear as day at this point, but there was only one thing to do now.

Fight.

Chapter 23

After hearing someone collapse to the ground, Vic moved down the line of cars—away from the action—until she reached the farthest car from the stairwell. Then she crawled forward to peek around its front tire to see what was happening.

What she saw made her stomach drop.

It was like the hotel room all over again, only Seba was in her position. Totally surrounded. And two of the guards who had left with her step-father were back.

Which meant he was back—probably just waiting at the top of the ramp with the other two for his men to get things right this time.

It felt so unfair to have Seba fighting them alone even though she knew she'd be useless. The best she could probably do would be to distract two of them by letting them carry her off while Seba took on the other four.

But then he'd just be distracted as he fought.

No, the only thing to do was hide. It's what he'd asked her to do, so that's what she would do while crossing her fingers that miracles happened more than once in a night.

A good fifty feet away, six men in suits surrounded Seba, who managed to look unconcerned as brass knuckles and telescoping batons came out of hiding.

"Shouldn't there be eight of you?" Seba asked, the echo of the structure carrying his words to her. "Three arrived with Vic, four came later, and two came after that. Am I counting right? Because, counting the guy on the ground, I'm missing two."

As if waiting to be summoned, the last two guards walked down the garage entrance.

"Ah, there they are!" Seba said, sounding pleased.

"Where is she, Archer?" Hawkins asked.

"Safe," Seba replied. "I know it's technically your job to keep her safe, but you're terrible human beings. So I'm taking over."

"Didn't take you for a talker," Hawkins said.

And, just like that, it was on—Bret swinging in with a steel baton first.

Vic pressed her face into her hands, unable to watch. She had no stomach for violence—especially when the odds were so uneven. More so when the person about to get hurt was trying to help.

Seba had shown up for her, and he was probably going to get killed for it.

He should have just run for it and left her. It wasn't like Evan wasn't going to get her in the end anyway. He wouldn't stop until he did.

Now Seba was about to be beaten to death, and it was all her fault.

Vic didn't realize she was crying until her eyes went wide at the sound of steel clattering across cement and she had to wipe tears away to clear the blur.

When she looked over and saw Seba still standing—one fist punching at a guard in front of him as Tristan swung at him with a rod from behind him.

Before Vic could cry out, the rod seemed to fall out of Tristan's hand—bouncing away—as he finished the swing of his strike, hitting nothing but air.

That was lucky!

A moment later, Seba pivoted and sent Tristan spinning with a punch. Vic watched him land on all fours and wobble as he tried to regroup.

Just then the elevator dinged and the fight kept on going as a couple stepped out—the man instantly putting himself between the woman and the fight. The woman responded by raising her phone up and filming as she was ushered away.

But Vic's eyes were drawn back to the fight when three men moved in on Seba at the same time from three different angles,

Vic didn't blink this time. She watched as the man who looked like a stack of muscles dodged each strike with a fluidity that looked impossible for his mass. Punches that looked like they should hit missed as Seba slipped past guards to land strikes of his own.

It was like watching a really violent ballet where only one person knew how to dance. She was so spellbound by it that she didn't notice Tristan getting up until he was already on his feet. Then he reached into his jacket. When his hand appeared again, there was a gun in it.

"No!" she screamed, unable to stop herself. But as he raised the gun, the magazine slipped out of the bottom a beat before the chambered bullet popped off to the side.

Even in the chaos, Vic heard the click of the dry fire as Seba knocked the third of three men to the ground in front of him.

Vic had no idea who this Seba guy really was, but he was taking down Evan Bauer's best security like he had a force field around him.

Suddenly, Vic was a much bigger fan of violence.

"Get 'em," she whispered under her breath.

Six were currently on the ground and three were still standing—Hawkins, Ellis, and Briggs, from the travel team. Briggs eyed one of the fallen batons then went for it, while Ellis seemed comfortable to stick with his fists, and Hawkins held back like he wanted to watch a little before choosing a new approach.

As Seba and Ellis went one-on-one, Briggs dove for the baton. Literally. One moment his legs were running and the next they locked like a bike tire with a stick shoved through its spokes. Since he was already bending, his head hit first, bouncing once before landing and sliding to a stop with the rest of him. He reached up and grabbed his face, body curling into a fetal position as Seba caught Ellis behind the chin and dropped him.

Only Hawkins remained standing and, after watching everything, he seemed to have the same idea as Tristan. He reached into his jacket like he was going for a gun, but then his hand stalled, moving twice under the fabric before coming out more slowly than it went in with no gun.

"You've got some interesting tricks up your sleeve," Hawkins said. "I'd be interested to know where you learned them."

"I've got a trick for you," Seba said walking toward him.

"Yeah?" Hawkins said, sounding unconcerned.

Seba charged him like a wrestler going for a takedown, but when Hawkins countered to meet him Seba went high again and kneed the man in the face before snaking his hand around to grab Hawkins by the collar.

"Yeah," Seba replied, looking like he was hooking his hands under the back of the man's tie. When he had a grip, he cranked it in a one-eighty. "It's called: Real Men Don't Wear Ties for Reasons."

Hawkins fought the choke, but once Seba kicked his knees out from under him, Hawkins faded quickly. Seba's free hand moved under Hawkins' jacket as he passed out, seeming to look for something, and coming out with a zip tie.

After Hawkins went limp, Seba waited an extra beat before dropping the man. Then he quickly bound Hawkins wrists behind his back, took a look around at all the men on the ground, and ran Vic's way.

"Vic!" he whisper-yelled. "Where are you?"

"Here!" she said, revealing her hiding spot next to the tire and ignoring the ache in her knees as she stepped away from the car.

Seba ran to her with what appeared to be honest concern. He'd just fought nine men and he was worried about *her*?

Vic's heart hammered as he approached. But, for the first time that night, the hammering wasn't out of fear. She wasn't quite sure what she was feeling, only that it tripled down when his thumbs swiped away the dampness on her cheeks as his eyes seemed to check her for injuries.

"Are you okay?"

Was *she* okay? Was he kidding? "Are *you*?"

He hesitated, his face clouding with confusion for a moment before he blinked the look away and nodded. "Somehow. Yes."

Vic had never wanted to be kissed more in her life. Nine men lay behind Seba on the concrete—some out cold, some gripping body parts—and all Seba had to show for it was a sheen of sweat.

There wasn't even a trickle of blood for her to wipe away as an excuse to touch him while he gazed at her like she was the only thing that mattered.

Her eyes dropped to his lips.

"Vic, are you sure you're okay?" he asked.

Definitely. She was definitely okay.

His hand came up to her chin and tipped her face up until they were eye-to-eye.

"Vic, will you—"

Yes! All day, yes!

"—follow me to the motorcycle? We've got to get out of here."

Oh. Yeah. That.

Also, a yes.

"Yeah," she sighed, holding on when his hand slid into hers.

"Let's go."

Chapter 24

What. Just. Happened?

Seba's mind spun, trying to figure out how he'd survived as he helped Vic with her helmet.

Later, he told himself. *Move now, figure things out later.*

Vic might not be the only one in shock at this point.

"This is your bike?" she asked from under the black visor.

"Yeah," he said, climbing on before he helping her do the same. "Your feet go there and you'll need to hold on when we get started. Okay?"

"Yeah," she breathed before climbing on and clinging tight.

It was both the best and worst thing that could have happened in that moment. Best because she felt perfect against him, but worst because now was not the time for anything to feel that good.

He had to keep his head in the game.

Bringing the motorcycle to life, Seba revved the engine several times, until the sound of it roared off every wall. Then he sped out, letting the wheels squeal as he made the two quick turns to the ramp and powered up, skirting the drop bar on his way to the street.

In his rearview mirror, he saw three of the guards already getting up. Then he was at street level and they were gone. He did see Evan's SUV, though, idling next to the curb with him alone inside like some toddler who needed the A/C on while he hung out in the back seat.

Seba flipped him the bird before turning right into traffic and letting his engine scream as he took another right at the next intersection and revved it again.

Vic held on like her life depended on it, her helmet digging into his back as Seba took the next intersection on a yellow light and pulled back on the engine, slowing dramatically as he approached the cover of some trees. He was about twenty feet off his mark when he heard another engine rev. It had a higher pitch, but Seba wasn't in a position to be picky.

When the other bike cut him off—tires squealing as it pulled in front—the passenger riding behind the driver flashed Seba a thumbs up. Seba barely had time to nod in return before making a hard right into a delivery entrance and aiming his bike for a ramp leading up into a white transport truck. He let momentum carry them up the ramp, not wanting to use the engine if he didn't have to.

Back on the street, the second motorcycle did something to earn some honks before roaring down the street and fading into the night.

Both tires on the level inside the truck, Seba killed the engine and walked the bike the rest of the way into position before kicking down the stand. Only then did he realize Vic was holding on to him like a human backpack.

He'd probably terrified her.

"We're done with that part," he said, giving her arm a reassuring pat. "Okay? We're done with the bike. You can take your helmet off."

"Dude!" a guy said as he hopped into the rear of the truck. "That timing was tight."

Seba tapped Vic's hands again. "I need you to let go. I've

got to talk to this guy."

That got her to release him and lean away, and Seba found himself annoyed with the loss of contact.

Head in the game, he told himself, pulling off his helmet as he unstraddled the bike.

"Jade won't stop until Chinatown, as promised," the guy said as Seba opened his saddlebag, grabbed his pack, and pulled an envelope out of the front pocket.

He handed the envelope to the guy. "Keep my baby safe. I'll pick her up Sunday."

The guy looked over the black leather and chrome and nodded with appreciation.

"I know how to transport precious equipment," he said, pulling out an envelope of his own. "Room 413."

The guy opened the flap at the top and gave the bills a quick flip through before offering his envelope in trade. "We're good."

By the time Seba looked back at Vic, she was staring at him like she'd landed on Mars and found a Willy Wonka factory.

"Last move," he said, holding out his hand her way. "We're almost at the finish line. All we need to do is find our room without being seen. You up for that?"

A mute nod was all he got before Vic's hand slipped into his and she followed him down the ramp.

Chapter 25

Vic stood in the hotel's shower, letting the water flow down her. Maybe she'd been in there ten minutes. Maybe it had been closer to thirty. She wasn't counting, nor did she want to.

She considered this shower an adult Time Out, and she'd get out when she was thinking straight again.

She'd kind of freaked out on Seba when they first walked into the room.

The hotel they'd just left was only a block away. Literally. A block.

Seba had explained all the reasons they were safe. Things like the other motorcycle drawing attention away to the other side of town, and being checked in under someone else's name, and the fact that no eyewitnesses could place them at the hotel—all combined with the fact that their current hotel's management would fight tooth-and-nail to keep her step-father's hounds from searching room-to-room.

His explanations made a shocking amount of sense, but only served to remind Vic that she didn't know why he was even helping her in the first place.

Her breakdown had started there, cascading with thoughts of worst-case scenarios until she'd decided to do what she always did and lean into the silver lining of one single, observable fact.

And right then—in that exact moment—the single, observable silver lining was: she was safe.

Whatever else might be, she was away from Evan and currently safe.

Maybe that would change later. Seba was a conman, after all. Maybe he'd fleece her or sell her to Russia, or do one of the other thousand things her terrified mind could drum up at the drop of a hat.

But, for now, he'd saved her. She was standing in a hot shower, and she was safe.

Seba had fought for her against insane odds and, now that he had her, he wasn't barging into the bathroom and laying down new rules.

Instead, he was on the computer, posting an ad trying to find a yacht they could use tomorrow to get them away from a city full of cameras that would recognize her.

One thing was for sure about Seba since he'd appeared on the scene: he hadn't planned for any of this. He was flying by the seat of his pants. And flying very well.

Given what she'd seen tonight, Vic could see why a man like him got paid the sums listed in his letters. It was still Day 1 and Vic would have paid him $100,000 for services rendered and call it a bargain.

Because she was alive … and might be sporting a bit of a crush in between freak outs. And that actually might have been part of her freak outs, if she was being honest—the terror of wanting to trust him enough to let herself feel something.

Vic still hadn't separated everything that had happened and how, but one of the things she kept seeing over and over was the look in his eyes when he'd informed her that she was in shock.

Something in the way he said it—with such calm … like he'd been there before … like it was familiar ground.

How had he known that watching his feet as they ran out of the building would fade into the background as she tried to remember everything else that happened? Like that slap of a hand on her forearm right before she hit the carpet.

Vic was remembering that part more and more clearly now. People might call her crazy if she said it out loud, and maybe she was, but someone had caught Vic that night.

She could remember putting her hands out when she started falling through the window, like she'd tripped and imagined her hands could break the fall. Not only had a hand clasped around her forearm in that moment, but she'd felt a pinch at the back of her neck.

Vic hadn't known what that meant until she came in for her shower and saw her mom's necklace missing.

It was the one heirloom she had. She wore it everywhere.

Now it was gone.

A small price to pay for her life, maybe, but her stomach sunk at the thought that she'd lost her mom's favorite necklace. It was pretty much the only thing the Bauer's let her have from her parents' estate. The rest was all in holding for someday when she was deemed capable of managing it herself.

What a joke.

Her whole life felt like a joke, now that she knew how close she had come to losing it.

What had she ever accomplished? Her parents had written songs that were still played on the radio. When people wanted to feel something, or send a love letter, or perform on a TV show, they reached for her parents' songs.

What had Vic done with her life?

Followed orders. That's what she'd done. Since day one. So unlike her parents, who had been total free spirits and music nerds—so lost in the music that they never looked up from their instruments to see the world around them.

That's how they'd met. They'd both gone to a songwriting jam session and by the time they both looked up to say, *'Hey, I like this song,'* everyone else had either gone home or gone to sleep.

Their relationship blossomed from there—heads bent over their guitars, trying to make a new sound.

Vic remembered how funny it had been to be a kid and see huge stars kiss up to her parents. Everyone wanted a song and they always thought some fancy gift or a case of wine would pave the way. Little did they know they were more likely to capture the hit-makers' attention with an embarrassing story or a weird question. Things like that would get Vic's parents sharing a look before sending them straight to the studio.

Vic was neither invited nor disinvited when they worked. Her mom and dad were so much in the zone that they didn't really notice if she was there either way. Vic could sing along or chime in with an instrument but she didn't have a gift that caught their ears.

They'd always been tuned in to each other when it came to music.

Then they'd signed with Bauer and within a year they'd become gaunt and forgetful. Everyone praised Vic's mom on how much weight she'd lost and how she had cheekbones to die for. They never mentioned how her skin was sallowing and that her joints were starting to jut.

Makeup and clothes could cover that up.

Besides, that's when the money had really started pouring in and people seemed more enamored with that.

When Vic was ten, they'd moved to a new house. It had been a party haven, and that's when things had gone downhill.

Vic didn't think about her parents very often these days. Mostly because it hurt, but also because nearly all her memories of them consisted of her watching them while they focused elsewhere. She had so many memories of seeing them happy but all those memories were tinged with the sense that she was unnecessary to their equation.

Her parents had needed each other, not her. She'd simply happened along the way.

It sucked.

Vic had never told anyone, but the morning she found them dead, she'd been mad at them. There they were, crashed out as usual, while she had no way to get to school. She'd let them sleep in but, after waiting as long as she could, she'd gone in.

When Vic reached out to wake them that morning, she'd pretty much been a brat about it. She couldn't remember what she said, only that her mom moved wrong when Vic pushed her.

It was the most vivid memory she had of her mom and something about that made Vic so angry.

She should have different memories. Everyone she knew who missed their parents had nostalgic memories, so why did she have *that* one?

She tried not to think about it ... just like she tried not to think about how she was now the poster girl for the lifestyle that had driven her to hide out in her bedroom every night for the last three years of her parents' lives.

She often wondered if Evan made her the poster girl of partying on purpose to mess with her.

Probably.

Or maybe he wasn't that smart and only knew how to promote one thing. Who knew?

Vic had never really let herself think about it before. Life with the Bauers had never been safe enough to reflect on anything but survival. Everything had been a dance of avoiding punishment.

What a waste.

It was amazing what a near-death experience and an hour in the shower could do when it came to spurring self-reflection.

Or maybe she'd actually only been in there five minutes and time was warped. Who knew? Vic sure didn't. All she knew was that the skin between her breasts and on her stomach was a bright red from the steady heat and that the carpet burns on her arm smarted when the water hit them.

The pain was a sharp reminder she was still alive as she tried to piece back together in her mind everything that happened that night.

Seba had said water helped process things. He'd also said to use the hotel soap because a new smell would help her find a new outlook.

How did he know?

When Vic had stepped into the shower, all her mind could do was relive the events leading up to the fall, over and over and over.

Now she was thinking about her parents and the musical babies they'd made together before giving them to others.

Looking back with an adult mind, Vic could see that they never meant to neglect her. They just didn't know what to do with a baby they had to keep. Then they'd leaned into chemicals to create, died with their minds lost in what they loved, and the rest was history.

Nothing she could do about it.

Not wanting to think about anything past that, Vic turned off the water and reached for a towel. The entire bathroom was a steam room but it felt good.

A light knock came on the door.

"I had some clothes delivered," Seba said through the door. "There's a shirt and shorts to sleep in right outside the door."

Washed clean, new smell—not a scent she was a fan of, but still … new smell— and now new clothes. The guy really knew how to cover the bases.

"Thanks," she replied, wrapping the towel around her so she could open the door.

When she poked her head out, Seba was on the computer again with a slight frown on his lips. It made for such an odd picture. He looked like such a meathead it was almost hard to

158

imagine he knew how to read. Guys like him watched sports while yelling at the screen. They didn't sit at computers in their spare time.

Right?

Vic shut the bathroom door again, keeping the steam in as she pulled on the blue tee and white drawstring shorts. Then she took some time blowing her hair dry until the steam was gone and she could see her makeup-less face in the mirror.

She should have asked him to pick up cosmetics while he was at it.

Oh, well. Someone had to see what she looked like without mascara sometime.

When she stepped out of the bathroom again, Seba looked up from his laptop. "Feeling better?"

Vic nodded and, surprisingly, meant it. She did feel better. She felt clean and her clothes were soft.

He pointed to a room service tray. "You said you wanted juice."

She had. She hadn't had anything since lunch and the adrenaline that kept her from feeling it had worn off.

"Thanks," she said, picking it up and nearly chugging it as she walked over to where he sat. "What are you doing?"

"Work stuff," he said evasively.

She stopped moving forward to give him space. "Oh, you don't need to tell me."

He shrugged. "It's not a huge deal. I planned to work other jobs this weekend and I kind of bailed on one today, so there's a little housekeeping to be done."

The word *housekeeping* sounded so strange coming from the guy who had just choked out Evan's right-hand man with his own tie.

That was her first thought. Her second was how close she'd really come to dying that day. If Seba had chosen to stick to his schedule...

"I'm basically done," he said, shutting the laptop and rising.

Without her shoes on, he seemed taller. And wider. And all she could remember was the feeling of holding on to that massive chest as he took her on the shortest motorcycle ride ever.

It had felt so good to hold onto something ... someone ... him.

Man, she was in serious trouble with this guy. It was literally his job to get people to fall for him and, as it turned out, Vic was no exception.

"Are you okay?" he asked, looking concerned.

If he was an actor, he was the best, because Vic really believed he cared. Worse than that, it made her want to ask for something she'd never asked for before ... something she shouldn't ask for, but something every part of her was begging for in synchronicity.

On any other day, she would have pushed the thought away. But, tonight, she needed it.

"Yeah," she said, putting the glass to the side. "Can I ask for a favor?"

"Sure," he said. No hesitation. It made her heart pound with hope.

Vic turned back to face him. "Can you hold me for a bit?"

It was one thing to feel her feet on the ground again and know she was physically safe. It was another to feel like someone didn't want to let go. And she needed that. With everything bubbling up in her right now, Vic really needed to lean in and believe someone cared enough to hold on.

Even if it was a lie.

"Sure," he said again, covering the distance between them and pulling her to him.

Vic wanted to thank him for not making her cover the distance but her mind quickly lost the will to form words as his hands found her back and her cheek pressed into the warm, firm pillow of his chest.

Man, the guy was a furnace. It felt nice.

She could also smell the remnants of the day on him and

realized she'd hogged the shower and he hadn't had a chance to clean up himself. She didn't mind, though. Seba might, but Vic kind of liked remembering snapshots of the night with every inhale. It made her feel safer, so she'd take it unless Seba said something.

All the while his hands moved lightly on her back, like he was trying to soothe a child to sleep. Before she knew it, she was doing it right back to him, her hands exploring his back over his shirt.

The mood could have shifted. It didn't. It simmered with all the things that could be. But within all those possibilities, there was really only one thing Vic wanted.

This. Exactly this.

To be held just like he was holding her. Nothing more, nothing less. His absolute wall of a chest holding steady while she leaned in and held on to a sense of stability ... of feeling safe.

Totally safe.

"Can we stay like this?" she dared to ask.

"Of course," Seba said, his voice rumbling through his chest as he made the impossible sound like the easiest thing in the world.

And somewhere in the middle of it all, Vic leaned in, inhaled the scent on his shirt, and fell asleep on her feet.

Chapter 26

When Vic Davalos held on, she held on. That's what Seba learned as he tried to take her to the bed farthest from the door so she could rest on her own.

But she was holding on in her sleep and he couldn't trick her into letting go without waking her. It was a dilemma because he didn't want to let her go either.

Vic still hadn't told him exactly what happened to her yet, but he knew for a fact that it involved going through a window and dropping one floor on a building that left no room for error. There were no ledges or ornamentation to hold onto on the exterior of the building.

Seba knew. He'd checked.

He'd also seen the window Vic had to pass through to land in the room. The pane had been missing from the frame—not part of it—all of it. Gone.

It was one of many inexplicable details of the night Seba couldn't reconcile as he stared at the ceiling in the dark.

Every so often, he could tell Vic was dreaming of falling. She'd fight and fidget against him in her sleep, then she'd go completely limp for about half a second before her right hand gripped into him and the rest of her shuddered.

She'd had the dream seven times by his count, always

settling back into a more relaxed sleep again after he rubbed his hand back and forth across her back a few times.

Seba hadn't found sleep himself yet. Given their current positions, he was a little terrified a sleeping-him might do something to destroy what little trust he'd built with her in some unconscious move. But it was good to be awake so he could think about tomorrow.

They had gotten away that night, but the sun would rise on a new day with new challenges.

Happily, Finder011 located a yacht Seba could rent for the day, but there was no way Seba was staying on the water after dusk, which meant he still needed options for tomorrow night.

Unless Vic had a plan for dealing with her step-father, they'd need somewhere off-radar for one more night. Then it would be Saturday and someone who signed their name with a blue flower seemed to think Vic would be safe by the time the sun went down.

Seba wasn't holding his breath on that one. Evan Bauer was a formidable enemy. Those he didn't own, owed him a favor. Bauer made sure of that.

Plus, the man had a spotless arrest record. He was Teflon, which meant he probably had some very high ups either in his debt or on his payroll. Seba had no doubt that if he and Vic ran to the police with the tale of what happened, no charges would be pressed, and they would find Evan waiting in the lobby when they tried to leave.

Then Seba would probably be arrested for assault, putting him in jail and Vic with Evan, and it would all be for nothing.

So Seba wouldn't be racing into anything.

Tomorrow was a think day. They'd go out on the water—away from people and technology—and see if nature had any inspiration to offer as they floated along.

When dusk came, he'd follow his gut to see where they'd go next.

He just had to keep sticking with his gut. Plans were for

city people—always projecting, with their need for control and perfection … always living in the future and chasing that next carrot.

Seba might live in a city, but he'd always be street. And street people committed to nothing but the moment because they knew the future had to survive the now.

One of his mentors had told him being street was like the story of the Three Little Pigs.

If Seba acted like the first little pig, and didn't take care of business when he had a chance, he'd have no cover when trouble came his way.

If he was like the second pig, and did things half-way, he'd end up fighting wolves with sticks.

If he wanted to survive, he had to work like the last piggy, making everything tight and solid, so that there was nothing for a wolf to do but move along or make a fool of himself huffing and puffing.

City people could be any type of pig they wanted. That was one of the luxuries of city life. Pigs that built with straw could make friends with others who made houses of brick and go running that way when there was trouble.

But it was everyone for themselves on the street. It was a different game, and Seba had to lean into his strengths if he was going to come out on top against a man like Evan Bauer.

Seba couldn't play Bauer's game; he had to make Bauer play his.

He had to figure out what that meant and what he had built that could withstand Bauer's blows because there was no way he was going to let that man have Vic back.

Not a chance.

Seba was pondering his options when he felt Vic start her dream cycle again. This time, after the half-second of freefall, her hand gripped and her breath froze.

She was awake.

"Someone caught me tonight," she said without preamble. "Those guys wedged me out that window and someone caught me like a trapeze artist out of nowhere."

Not knowing what else to do, Seba gave her back a light rub. "Okay."

She grew still. "You believe me?"

Seba nodded in the dark. "I keep thinking about the fight. There were at least five times I should have been dead or close to it. And every time, something impossible happened to stop it. Some stuff I saw tonight was no less crazy than an invisible trapeze artist."

Vic was still for another moment. "I saw a few things during the fight, too."

She had? "Like what?"

"Like ... when Tristan's gun unloaded itself before he could fire. That was weird."

He was both fascinated and nauseated that he'd missed such a pivotal moment. "I didn't see that."

"He was behind you," she explained. "Ready to shoot you in the back."

"That tells you a lot about the man," Seba said through his teeth, fighting back a sudden flare of anger. "I'm really glad that's not how I left this world. I would have been really mad about that."

She didn't say anything. It was his first warning that he'd overshared.

"I'm pretty sure I ruined your life tonight," she said against his chest.

Seba tilted his head up, trying to get a look at her expression, but it was too dark. "Why would you say that?"

"You were on the computer earlier trying to smooth things over with clients," she said, sounding sad and tired. "But after tonight, Bauer will make sure you never work in this town again. He'll probably even put a hit out on you."

Seba let himself laugh. "Only a fool would take that job."

She didn't laugh along. "Seba, I'm serious."

"Me, too."

The room was impossibly silent in the next few moments.

Seba didn't even hear her breathe.

"Look, Vic," he said. "I know it seems like Bauer owns the world, but there's a whole other stratosphere out there where people would choose a bag of dirt over a partnership with Evan Bauer. Trust me."

"But you'll never live or work in any big city again," she said, her voice shivering with what sounded like incoming tears.

"I'll live anywhere I want," he replied, giving her back another reassuring rub. She seemed to like it. "Maybe I'll keep living here just to piss him off. I've been waiting to take on someone like him my whole life, but I'm way too small a player to be taken seriously if I punch up at him. But if he wants to make me relevant by punching down and declaring me an enemy, it's game on."

"But first you'll lose your career!"

"So I'll find another one," he said with a shrug. "I'm not exactly a one-trick pony."

"No one will hire you."

"So I'll get a job where no one needs to hire me."

She shook her head against his chest. "That doesn't even make sense."

"Sure, it does."

She propped herself up on his chest and he saw the silhouette of her staring him down but nothing else. "Name one scenario where you still have a career after helping me with my step-father."

"Hmm," Seba said, thinking through the options. "Well, you may not know this, but I am awesome at making forgeries."

"Forgeries?"

"Yeah. Fakes," he said. "And people always want to buy them. So, if Bauer fully blacklists me, maybe I'll live the dream and finally open a gallery. Los Angeles loves its galleries."

"A gallery of forgeries?" she said, sounding skeptical.

"Sure," he mused. "It's how Michelangelo got his start. Why not me? I'll put everything on sale for six months, make bidding private, and the highest bidder wins."

A beat of silence, then, "You're joking."

"Kind of," he admitted. "But now that I'm thinking about it, it seems like it might be fun. I could even name the gallery Blacklisted and put it right downtown. Then I can watch to see which of Bauer's supposed allies buys from me in secret."

"I can think of a few who might just for spite," Vic murmured.

Good. She was playing along.

"From there, I can find the splits in his loyalties," Seba continued. "Those will lead me to the cracks in his kingdom. Then I'll start going after what he cares for most—money—making it fall through his hands, back to the customers he so despises, while I innocently go about my business selling forgeries."

A short pause, then, "He would hate that."

Seba grinned in the dark. "I know."

"No. I'm serious. He would try to kill you for making him look bad."

"And I'd catch him every time and capture it with film and art," he said with a shrug. "Sales would skyrocket. I could even make a gallery of all his attempts in the main entrance entitled, #OMGWhyAreYouSoObsessedWithMe?"

Vic's entire body shook with laughter. After everything that happened that night, it felt good to know she could still laugh.

It felt better to be the one who made her laugh.

When the laughter faded, she relaxed against him again. "Well, if you were trying to make me feel better about you losing your livelihood, you succeeded. I actually want you to get blacklisted now."

"Well, let's not get ahead of ourselves," he said. "The weekend's not over. I might still have a career."

"Don't bet on it," she said, sounding deflated again. "Neither of us has one anymore."

Seba scrunched his face in disbelief, but she didn't see it in the dark. "Are you kidding? You don't need Bauer for anything. You must have all sorts of ideas for things you'd do if he wasn't at the driver's wheel."

She seemed hesitant. "Only one, really."

"What's that?"

"It's not going to happen," she deflected.

"Well, it's not if you can't say it out loud," he countered. "What is it?"

"I ..."

"Yes?" he prompted.

"I ... actually want to be a designer," she said in a rush. "I have the name picked out and everything, but there's no—"

"What's the name?" he asked before she could go full Debbie Downer on herself.

"It's stupid..."

"Best not to drag it out then," he teased.

He felt, more than heard, her sigh in frustration. "You can be a pain sometimes, you know that?"

"I literally get paid for the skill," Seba said with a smile. "What's the name of your designing business?"

A quick, annoyed huff, then, "Ria Designs."

"Ria?" he said, testing the name on his lips. "Why Ria?"

"It's ... like this whole thing with my name," she said in a nervous ramble. "Like, when I was young, my parents always called me by my full name, Victoria, to remind me to be victorious. Then I went to the Bauers and they turned me into Vic, the bad girl who sells Bauer's crap. So I always thought that when I got a chance to be myself, that I'd want to rebrand myself 'Ria' and tell the full story of my name and how I went from Vic-to-Ria."

"Victoria," he smiled, catching the vision. "Your victory is how you went from Vic to Ria."

"It's stupid, right?"

He shook his head in the dark. "That might be one of the coolest life goals I've ever heard. If it doesn't happen, I'm going to be very upset."

She let out a little laugh before ending on a sour note. "It won't be happening anytime soon, though."

"Why not?" he asked.

"Because I suck at designing."

"Says who?" he pressed.

"Says Instagram." She sounded dejected. "I've been posting for over a year and exactly no one finds me interesting."

Something clicked in Seba's mind. "On Instagram?"

"Yes," she replied.

"On your phone?"

"Uh, yeah. That's where people look at Instagram."

"Hmm. Then you should probably know that your step-father installed a program on your phone that turns your Instagram account to 'private' anytime you close the app. No one can see you exist unless you're looking at it on your phone."

She went completely still. "No way."

"Yes way," he replied.

She rolled away from him, grabbing the spare pillow on the bed and screaming into it. Then she threw it against the wall.

"I knew it," she seethed. "I told myself I was being paranoid, but I knew he was doing something like that. Because some of my designs are solid *gold*!"

"I thought you sucked," he teased.

"I'm awesome," she countered in a pout. And he believed her.

"Well, I'm glad we got that straightened out," he said, sitting up. "Now, if you don't mind, I'm going to go over to the next bed and I think we both should try for some sleep."

"You ... don't have to," she said, a definite undercurrent

of an invitation to stay where he was in her tone.

"I do," he said, getting up. "We've got to be smart here. When things get intense, it's easy to be distracted—or, rather, it's easy to *want* to be distracted. But if we're going to get through this, we need to keep our heads as much in the game as Evan is. We need to stay smart and keep our focus. I already know from experience that I become very dumb when I kiss you. So nothing even close to that will be happening this weekend, okay?"

A beat of silence, then, "Okay."

Man, he wished he could see her face when she said that one word. Her tone was totally unreadable and he was suddenly quite invested in hearing her admit she felt the same.

But he didn't force it.

"Good night," he said instead.

"Good night," she replied.

And neither said another word for the rest of the night.

Chapter 27

Based on the sun's position, Vic guessed it to be about 2:00. She was supposed to be at a commercial fitting at 2:00. A new bra was launching and she was one of the three women who made the cut to model.

And she was missing her fitting.

Nora was probably freaking out but Vic couldn't bring herself to care. She was floating in the middle of the ocean somewhere, half-asleep in the sun.

At first, the lift and drop of the yacht had reminded her of the night before. Of falling. Then the rhythm had become soothing … a constant reminder that she'd been caught— both during the fall and after.

One of her saviors last night had let her go; the other had not. He was risking it all and dropping large sums of money to keep her safe.

Vic had seen the cash hand off the night before with the truck driver and, again, this morning when he put a large packet in a lockbox on the dock.

Never a word about it. He just did it.

If Seba didn't end all this by selling her at an auction across the border, what he was doing now would easily be the kindest thing anyone had done for her in her life.

He was making the world disappear without asking for it to revolve around him in exchange. He was around—probably in the captain's seat watching the water—but giving her space.

'You have a lot to process,' he'd said before they set out to sea. *'Today is your day to relax. Take it. After this, we're on the move again.'*

So it had been a quiet day.

She'd slept a lot, dreaming every time. Some of the dreams were memories, some were random, some were actually hopeful.

Seba's revelation about her Instagram settings was a game changer—not that she needed the world's approval to chase her dream.

Okay, maybe she did, a little.

But this was her life. If she wanted to put everything she had into designing clothes while trying her hand at being a philanthropist, that was her prerogative.

She hadn't told Seba about her whole business model the night before. She'd kind of been sidetracked by how Evan had used her insecurities to play her yet again.

Well, Vic was officially done with all that—done with letting think tanks, calculated ROIs, and polls decide her future. If she got a second chance at the end of all this, she was going for it.

Almost dying was at least good for something: perspective. Vic had a lot of it now and the only question in all of it was whether she wanted to go through the effort of removing Seba from her updating fantasies or letting them play out.

The man might be giving her space on the yacht, but every time Vic closed her eyes, there he was. At her side … cheering her on … scowling at men who looked too long … holding her hand like she belonged … kissing her like no one was watching, even when they were.

He was even in her designs now. Vic had always had

mixed feelings about how to handle ties when it came to women's suits.

Keep them? Ditch them? Leave one button unbuttoned and the tie untied?

But after watching Seba choke out Hawkins last night while taunting that real men didn't wear ties, Vic had updated opinions. With her designs, there would be only two acceptable tie options: untied or tied loosely enough to slide over the head, and not tightened once around the neck.

It was weird how things like that came into focus the more time she spent with him—how the chaos in her mind just ... resolved and relaxed.

All her life, Vic had never felt like she fit in anywhere. Everyone always called her pretty and told her how lucky she was, but she'd never felt like anyone really saw anything beyond that.

And they were *always* making moves. Vic wasn't sure if she'd ever gone this long without someone making a move on her.

She hadn't even caught Seba looking.

It was almost offensive.

Yes, he was crazy hot and probably had women throwing themselves at him all the time, but Vic actually got paid to be hot and he seemed to be making no effort to notice.

He did mention their kiss last night, though.

Vic smiled at the memory, letting it play over the glow of sunlight passing through her eyelids as she basked in the sun. It was one of the few things Evan had commanded her to do that she didn't regret.

That kiss...

"Got everything you need?" Seba said, interrupting her thoughts.

Vic sat up with a jerk just in time to see Seba place some sunscreen on the table next to her.

"More juice?" he added. "Water? Actual food this time?"

Squinting against the sunlight, Vic held up her water

bottle. "All set."

"Okay," he said, starting away. "I'll let you get back to it."

She hesitated, a question tickling in the back of her mind. "One thing?"

He turned back, looking ridiculously chiseled in his board shorts. "Yeah?"

Vic almost forgot her question. And when Seba caught her staring at his chest, she almost lost the courage to ask it.

"Yes?" he repeated.

"Can I ask you something?" she fumbled.

"Of course," he replied.

"What's..." Oh, man, she felt stupid. "What's your full name? You go by Seba, but what's your name? Like, on your birth certificate?"

He frowned at the question, clearly not comfortable with it, before taking a breath and seeming to shrug the frown away.

"Sebastian," he said. "Sebastian Kahn."

Then he walked back up to the captain's seat.

Sebastian, she thought with a smile. That fit him somehow.

And Kahn? Oh, that definitely fit. It was like the sound other men heard in their heads when Seba punched them.

Kahn!

Vic smiled as she relaxed back into the lounge chair, not even fighting it when the seventh-grader in her mind whispered, *Ria Kahn.*

That was totally the name of a designer. A sassy one who didn't take lip and marched to her own drum. Vic would have to cut her hair to pull off a name like that—something with style and body. Maybe something like the Captain Marvel look in her suit.

That would be so cool.

It probably wouldn't happen, but whatever. Today was her day for dreaming so she'd dream whatever she wanted. If only for the day.

For the moment, Vic was willing to believe she'd kind of earned it.

Chapter 28

Seba was securing the yacht to the dock when he felt eyes watching him. Not a passing gaze or a lingering look at his muscles while they worked. Not even the assessing glance of someone paid to care who came and went on the marina.

He felt the scrutinizing gaze of someone very interested in details.

Seba peered in the direction of the attention and saw a teenage girl standing at the edge of the dock with her camera raised in his direction.

Then he felt another pair of eyes.

Another woman, this one on a docked boat three rows down. She was watching him from the railing.

Him. Not Vic. He'd told her to wait inside the cabin for exactly this reason: they didn't need people looking their way.

So what was with the stares?

The next time the woman at the railing caught Seba's eye, he saw her phone was raised, too.

Two women watching him, two women taking pictures.

What had happened while they were out at sea?

Too much, apparently.

Knowing they needed to get a move on, Seba walked

back to the ladder to climb up and found a business card balancing on one of the rungs.

It had not been there before.

He picked it up, noting it was for a Mexican restaurant in Ventura, before flipping it over and spotting a blue flower he'd seen once before.

Above the flower, someone had written: *If you need a place to hide out tonight, visit this restaurant between 8-10 pm. You can trust them.*

He flipped the card over again, listening hard for inner-warning bells to chime. He had no idea who this Blue Flower person was, but nothing churned in his gut when he imagined accepting the offer.

If it was just him, he'd take the offer in a beat. But with Vic in tow, he was second-guessing everything.

He pocketed the card and climbed up the ladder.

"Vic?" he called out, feeling a sense of relief when she immediately appeared.

"Yeah?" she said, her smile relaxed and bright. The sight of her looking refreshed and maybe even a little happy had him catching his breath, but he didn't have time to dwell on it.

"We've gotta go," he said. "We've got eyes on us."

Her smile faded. "But I stayed below deck—"

"Not you," he said before she could finish. "Me. For some reason, they're looking at me, and I need to get you somewhere safe while we find out why."

"Oh," she said, moving forward and reaching for his hand in an unprompted gesture that had him feeling more protective than ever. He checked to see if either of the women were watching.

Both were.

He had to get Vic out of here before someone posted something online and all of Team Bauer descended on the location.

Not knowing what else to do, Seba pulled out his phone

and redialed the last number he'd called.

"You're becoming a regular," DHack said as he picked up. *"What is it this time?"*

Just then, Seba felt a new pair of eyes start to track him. Something was definitely up.

He led Vic toward the ladder. "Got another driver who wants to make some quick cash?"

"I've got one right here."

Chapter 29

Seba wasn't quite sure why he took the leap and told DHack's driver to take them to Ventura, only that it felt right.

When the driver asked where to drop them, Seba did another gut check and gave him the address.

As much as he wanted to be suspicious of the blue flower, the survivor in Seba seemed to trust the seal so far, even if his mind had its arguments about following no one's lead but his own.

Vic spent most of the ride using her new phone to figure out why they had been spotted so quickly. Apparently, Seba had gone viral over the past twenty-four hours.

The woman who had gotten off the hotel elevator the night before had filmed most of the fight and even caught the moment Seba ran over to grab Vic at the end, along with their noisy departure.

Her original post was captioned, *So THIS happened @ my hotel 2nite. Am I crazy or is that Vic Davalos at the end?*

The post had been retweeted over 750,000 times and there were tons of comments and theories.

Once that mystery was solved, Vic found the pictures of them returning to the marina an hour earlier—Seba glaring territorially at the camera as he held her hand. It made for quite an image and the tabloids had run their own narrative.

Davalos Falls for Grifter, Goes on Reckless Rampage.

Apparently, Vic had been volatile for weeks now and "close friends" were nervous about her increasingly erratic behavior since meeting L.A.'s most infamous bad-boy hustler. A few articles mentioned the shoe-burning incident at the club, making it sound much more dramatic than it was.

"So that's how they're handling it," Vic had murmured to herself while reading through the headlines. And that's all she'd said about that … as if she'd expected nothing less and maybe a whole lot more.

She'd spent most of the ride to Ventura scrolling through comments and fan accounts to see what they were saying.

Not sure what he could do to make things better, Seba let Vic focus on the phone while he ran scenarios of how to keep them safe if their final destination turned out to be a dead end or trap.

By the time they stood in the transport truck's rearview mirror, it was 8:27 p.m. and the restaurant was thirty feet away.

He could either go in or improvise from here. His mind said to detour; his gut said to go in, and Vic's grip on his hand told him she trusted him either way.

Decision time. No pressure.

From the outside, he could see the restaurant was relatively busy, with maybe thirty people inside. All Latin. And when Seba watched their mouths, he saw Spanish, not English, on their lips.

Their body language looked right—casual and comfortable—like they were normal people chilling on a Friday night.

Seba made his decision and looked into Vic's nervous face. "Ready to check this place out?"

She adjusted her grip—her fingers threading into his. "Wherever you go, I'm coming with you."

Okay, she really needed to not say things like that. It

made his heart beat funny and his mind definitely want to take a detour. But it was 8:27 p.m., and people had their eyes open for both him and Vic. If this restaurant was willing to hide them for some reason, Seba needed to accept the offer.

"Let's go," he said, and led her in.

Loud conversations filled the air as they entered—all Spanish and casual. But the jovial mood quieted in a ripple as the guests took note of them walking in. Within five seconds, the room was silent.

Seba scanned the many faces watching back—most uncertain, some unfriendly, a few more genuinely scared. Glances swapped around the room, all of them landing on the same man at least once—a guy in his twenties, sitting with two other men at the far corner table like it was an unofficial office.

Seba guided a now-hesitant Vic their direction.

The two "friends" stood up protectively as they approached and Seba responded by holding up the business card for them to see. Maybe it would mean something to them, maybe it wouldn't, but it sent the signal he was there for a distinct reason.

The men glanced at their boss, who kept his eyes on Seba and nodded that the approach was okay.

Vic's other hand snaked around his forearm nervously as they reached the table and he gave her hand a squeeze to let her know they were okay.

It was quiet as a church in the restaurant when Seba placed the business card down on the table in front of the man.

"Someone gave me this today." Seba said, sticking to English. He spoke Spanish fluently, but habit had him keeping that to himself in case things weren't as they seemed. "Does this mean something to you, or should I keep going?"

The man's eyes narrowed in confusion as he picked the card up, glanced at the front and flipped it over to the back. Then his eyes flared slightly and he pulled out his phone.

A moment later, he had someone on the line.

"I'm looking at a blue flower," the man said in Spanish. *"Just like your tattoo."*

There were a few beats of silence, then he hung up and stood.

"You didn't see anything," he said to the restaurant in Spanish, then motioned to Seba and Vic and switched to English. "You two. Follow me."

Then everyone started talking again as Seba and Vic were led to a utility van.

Chapter 30

Vic's hand locked into Seba's as they rode in the back of a windowless van to the soundtrack of *Bailando*. After that, *Vivir Mi Vida* played. Two of the men from the restaurant rode in the front while the third watched over Seba and Vic in the back. No one spoke.

The path to their destination was blocked as they drove, but Seba didn't need to see to make a mental map back to their starting point. He instinctively tracked time, approximate speed, distance, and turns as they made their way to the second location.

These guys might pass Seba's gut check, but he was never above knowing where his exits were.

When the van came to a stop and the engine turned off, live music replaced the radio. Somewhere outside the van, a mariachi band was playing. The music's volume tripled when the passenger got out and opened the van's rear doors.

Then the music was joined by one of Seba's favorite aromas in the world.

"Carne asada," he said in reflex, inhaling deeply.

Vic pulled a different face at the smell but seemed amused by his reaction. "A favorite?"

"Oh, yeah," he said, holding out his hand to help her out.

If the fates were kind, they were headed in the direction of food. Seba hadn't had a full meal in days.

"This way," the guy from the restaurant said in English before walking toward the side gate of a home that glowed with lights from the backyard.

The two sidekicks waited for Seba and Vic to follow, closing the van's doors behind them and bringing up the rear as Seba and Vic followed the leader to the backyard.

Vic's hand didn't leave his, her other hand reaching across her body and gripping his forearm again as they walked through a dark side-yard to the party in the back.

The fates were indeed being kind. Behind the unassuming house, a full-on fiesta was in full swing.

In a flash, Seba was transported back to his childhood, where parties like this happened on rooftops or in apartments back in New York. His mom had taken him a few times and he spent the night playing video games, drinking endless cans of Pepsi, and letting the *abuelas* heap his plate with more rice and tacos and carne asada than he could ever eat in a week.

Fiesta nights were the best nights.

So when Seba stepped into the backyard, with its festoon lighting, colorful decorations, and mismatched lawn chairs, he felt oddly at home.

To the far left, three picnic tables separated the food into offerings of meats, sides, and desserts, with coolers for drinks set at the end.

Straight ahead was the mariachi band—a group of men playing together like they'd been doing it all their lives while middle-aged couples and young children danced in an open area of grass.

This was a family event, Seba realized. All ages, multiple families. Conversations in both English and Spanish as people laughed and joked.

Their host was taking a huge risk letting Seba and Vic come here. Realizing that, Seba's trepidation came down several more notches.

No one here intended them harm. It was he and Vic who had to prove they weren't here to ruin the night.

Off to the side of the dancing area, a huddle of girls who looked like they might be in high school eyed Vic like they recognized her. They tapped shoulders and whispered—eyes wide like they didn't believe who they were seeing—while the band played on.

Unlike at the restaurant, nearly everyone ignored their arrival, lost in their own worlds and good time.

On instinct, Seba scanned the crowd, looking for the person who had been on the other side of the phone back at the restaurant.

A person with a blue flower tattoo.

No one fit the bill.

The two sidekicks from the restaurant moved past on Seba's side and gestured for Vic and him to follow. "C'mon. Grab some food. Make yourself at home."

Vic looked up at him, as if waiting for Seba to confirm this was really what they were doing.

He gave her hand a squeeze and nodded. "We're safe here. Our host probably wants to watch us for a bit to check us out. Let's go eat."

Vic looked hesitant and her feet didn't move with him when he stepped forward.

Seba paused. "What is it?"

"I, um, none of this food is on my diet. I don't think I can eat it."

Seba had to fight not to roll his eyes. She hadn't even seen the food yet. How could she know if it was on her diet?

"All you've had over the past twenty-four hours are smoothies and juice," he said. "Your body needs food. Forget about the calories for one night and *eat.*"

She still looked uncertain, but this time she walked with him as he moved forward.

Halfway to the food, the *abuelas* intercepted them, guiding them to the food tables and loading plates as they went on about how Vic needed to put on weight and strong men needed to eat.

Seba heaped his plate with tacos, Brazilian hot dogs, and carne asada. Vic fought valiantly to limit her plate to beans and rice but still got a taco in the mix. Then they were handed Tecate to drink and Seba led Vic to an empty table for four.

People could sit with them if they chose, but Seba wasn't going to crash anyone else's night and force them to play nice.

Everyone was laughing and dancing, most genuinely not even noticing their arrival, except the teenage girls. They were getting bolder with their looks and Vic had gone so far as to wave at them, which seemed to send the girls into a tighter huddle to decide what to do next.

Two minutes later, all five of them were standing around Vic and Seba's the table.

"Are you Vic Davalos?" their ringleader asked, as if Vic might actually be an imposter.

Vic smiled up at them. "Yeah. I am."

The ringleader regarded Seba next. "And you're the guy from the video."

It wasn't a question.

"Oh, my gosh!" one of the other girls squealed, taking one of the two extra seats. "Tell us everything! They say you've been tearing up hotel rooms for weeks and setting things on fire."

"That was one pair of shoes," Vic said defiantly. "And they were cutting into my ankles like you wouldn't believe."

"So you burned them on a bar?" the ringleader asked, still sounding skeptical.

"Yes," Vic said with just as much attitude and, for some reason, that seemed to break the ice.

"Epic," one of the girls gushed as they all reached for seats to sit around the table.

Seba suddenly felt very out of place as all the girls leaned in like it was gossip time at a lunch table.

"Now, seriously," the second girl said, leaning forward. "Tell us everything. Like, what does a white girl have to do to turn the media against her? They are *so* after you right now!"

Vic looked up at Seba like she wasn't sure how to respond.

Seba shrugged. "Tell them whatever you're comfortable sharing."

"It's that juicy?" another gushed. "Dish up. It's not anything we haven't heard before."

"Or done before," another snickered.

One pointed at Seba. "Is he your boyfriend?"

Vic hesitated. "No. He's my bodyguard."

That earned a collective, "Whaaat?" intermixed with a few, "*Que?*"

"No way," the ringleader said, looking between them. "It's more than that."

Behind the girls, someone stepped out of the patio door and caught Seba's eye. She was small, clear-skinned, and a tomboy sort of beautiful in her jeans and a soccer jacket. Seba guessed her to be in her late twenties, but it was hard to tell.

"There's not," Vic was saying. "I've only known him two days."

"Wait. You met him *yesterday?*"

Seba kept listening with one ear as he watched the woman in the background. Her eyes were steady as she looked over the gathered crowd, making sure everyone was doing well. Then she went to check on the food.

"Yes," Vic stammered. "I mean, well, we met for like five minutes two years ago. But we met again yesterday."

Everything about the background woman was measured. It was she who placed a comforting hand on the *abuelas,* rather than the other way around.

"And who was he fighting last night?"

"Those were my guards."

The woman finished scanning the tables, then moved to the coolers to make sure they were stocked.

"Wait," the ringleader said as he kept watching. "So why was this bodyguard fighting your other bodyguards?"

"Yeah," another girl chimed in. "Why?"

"Well … um, because the other guys were told to hurt me, and he stepped in to stop them."

"Seriously?"

The woman in the background started talking to a young family at one of the tables. Everyone looked up at her with smiles. With respect.

"That's messed up," one of the teens said.

"And kind of hot," decided one of the others.

The woman in the background moved on from the family, glancing Seba's way in passing as she went. When her eyes landed on him, he was waiting. They locked gazes and he sent her a nod of acknowledgment.

She nodded back.

"Excuse me," Seba said, standing from the table. "Can you ladies watch Vic for a moment? I need to speak with someone."

All the replies came on top of each other.

"Yes!"

"Of course!"

"Totally!"

"Yes!"

"Are you kidding?"

Nodding his thanks, Seba gave Vic's shoulder a little squeeze. "I'll stay in sight."

She looked unsure, but nodded. "Okay."

Then Seba walked over to where the resident Alpha waited for him.

Chapter 31

The woman's name was Isa.

She and Seba took a seat at the table the farthest from the band and were immediately served two Tecates by someone who disappeared as quickly as they arrived.

The first thing Isa wanted to see was the business card.

"Do you know who this is?" Seba asked, handing it over.

She sent him a surprised look. "Don't you?"

Seba shook his head. "Nope. But they're acting like a friend."

Isa nodded. "That's good for you, then. Enemies of this guy don't fare very well in the end."

Seba's gaze instinctively went to Vic, who was looking back with an expression he hadn't seen before. He didn't have time to analyze it.

"He seems to want Vic alive," Seba said, turning back to Isa. "He paid me, in advance, to protect her through tomorrow."

Her head tilted as if that didn't make sense. "And what about after tomorrow?"

Good question. If Vic wasn't safe, Seba didn't plan on going anywhere without her, but he also knew they couldn't run forever.

He had to find a solution.

"For now, it's about keeping her safe," he said, knowing he was skirting the question but not having a better answer.

"Well, you're both safe here for the night," Isa said. "But if trouble is chasing you, it's probably best you move on in the morning. This is a neighborhood with kids and we just got it cleaned up. I'd prefer to keep heat off these streets."

Seba nodded. "Agreed. Tonight is plenty. Thank you."

"Don't thank me," she said, giving the card a little wave before handing it back to him. "I'd be dead if it wasn't for this guy. I owe him everything, including the money he let me walk away with. If he needs a favor, he gets a favor. No offense, but staying here has nothing to do with you. If he told me to kick you out, I'd kick you out. That's how it is."

"No questions asked?"

"No questions asked."

That was interesting. What kind of man inspired such loyalty?

"How often does he ask you for favors?" Seba asked.

Isa eyed him as if debating whether to answer before deciding to share. "It's been three years since he helped me, and you're the first favor he's asked."

"Did he tell you we were coming?"

Isa shook her head. "Nope. So imagine my surprise when you two rolled up. I was half-expecting the Hiltons to get out of the van after you."

Seba laughed. "Yeah. I'll bet."

Isa looked across the bustling yard to where Vic and the teens were talking. "It's funny, if you'd asked those girls an hour ago if they liked Vic Davalos, they would have sworn she was a white devil. Now they're swooning."

"She's a good person," Seba said, ignoring how his heart tugged at the truth of it.

Isa studied him for a moment. "I saw your video. Nine against one? What was that about?"

Seba's heart hammered lightly at the memory and he

decided to cut right to the chase. "They threw her off the hotel and I was making sure they didn't get another chance."

Her eyebrows shot up. "How did she survive that intact?"

Seba shook his head. "No clue. They threw her out on the seventh floor and somehow she landed on the sixth."

Isa let out a low whistle. "Sounds like she has an angel looking out for her."

"Or something," Seba said, deciding not to mention the whole invisible trapeze-artist angle.

Isa studied Vic from a distance for a moment, her dark eyes serious. "What does she need?"

Seba let out a puff of air. "Man, I've been asking that for a while now and I'm not sure. Maybe for people to believe her? Or to have her back? I mean, it's easy to hate people in her position. I get it. I've done it plenty of times." He'd even done it to Vic while trying to avoid her. "It can kind of be a team sport to watch stars fall. But if that happens in this case, the bad guy definitely wins. And that's what he's counting on, so … yeah, given who she is, I really don't know of a foolproof way to help her."

Isa frowned, leaning back in her seat and taking a sip of her beer as she thought. Something sparked in her eyes that Seba recognized. It was the glint of a head boss scrolling through her mental Rolodex of arsenal.

Isa wasn't merely the Alpha of some organized neighborhood. She had a crew.

"I think I know why *he* sent you here," Isa said after several moments.

Seba leaned forward, eager for options. "You think you can help her?"

Isa shook her head. "Not her. You. I see why he wanted you to meet me."

Seba leaned back again. "Me?"

"You," she said, looking him up and down. "What do you do? I've got a hundred bucks that says you're dodging your potential and wasting your talents chasing money."

Well, that was specific.

"And I'll save you from telling me I'm right," she said with a wink. "We both know I am. I know who I saw in that video, just like you pegged who I was while I was still halfway out of view. No one's ever done that before, by the way. Only you."

She took another drink and let him sit with that.

"You felt me notice you?" he asked.

"Don't you feel it when people notice you?" she countered.

Yes. He did. But how did she know?

"You don't act like a bodyguard," she accused. "Bodyguards are vigilant. They don't trust their surroundings, but you walked back here, scanned the place once and told your girl she was safe. And she believed you."

Well, Vic wasn't his girl. It seemed like a petty thing to point out, but a selfish thing to let slide.

He let it slide.

"And now my nephew is inside trying to throw his deejay set together to impress Vic while five girls who scream against cultural appropriation are trying to teach her how to dance *zapateado*." Isa smiled off in Vic's direction and Seba followed the line of her gaze to see that Vic was, in fact, dancing. "Your girl makes friends fast. I know that because my girls don't."

That got a smile out of Seba.

"But back to you," Isa said. "The Pimpernel chose you to watch over Vic for a reason. And I think that's the same reason he brought the two of you to my door."

There was something uncomfortable about Isa's gaze, so he ignored it—focusing on taking a drink instead. "Pimpernel? That's what this guy goes by?"

She nodded. "Cobalt Pimpernel, to be exact. Once upon a time, he found me where I ought not to be, doing what I ought not be doing. Turns out, I was the most innocent person in my group, but that's not saying much, all considered. He could have thrown me out with the rest of the trash, but he gave me the Mufasa speech instead."

Smiling, Seba threw up air quotes. *"You are more than what you have become.* That one?"

"That's the one," she agreed. "Then he gave me a business card and told me to look the guy up."

Before Seba could respond to that, Isa stood.

"Wait here. I have something for you. I'll be right back." Then she went into the house.

Seba turned his attention back to Vic, who immediately sensed him watching and smiled back as she danced. She looked like she was having fun which made Seba feel like maybe he'd done something right in all this.

Vic was happy. She was dancing. She was smiling at him, making him feel like his heart was somersaulting in his chest. It was a dangerous feeling he needed to keep an eye on.

She motioned for him to join her.

Not a chance.

The day Seba danced with Vic Davalos would be the day he went full-stupid for her, and this was not that day.

She doubled-down on her request and he indicated he was waiting for Isa.

Vic frowned and broke eye contact, turning her attention back to the teens right as Isa returned and handed over a leather-bound book. It looked pretty old.

"Whoa, are you sure you want to part with this?" he asked, testing its materials against his hands. Leather cover. Hemp paper. Hand-written text. It would be a doozy to forge. "Looks valuable."

She waved that off. "Books aren't meant to be stored. One day, you'll meet someone who needs it and you'll pass it on, too. I would teach you like I was taught, but I think you already know most of it. You just need to put it in order."

Seba leafed through the pages, recognizing a diagram he'd seen years ago on one of them. "Hey, I've seen this before!"

"Yeah?" Isa said, only looking half-surprised.

He held the book toward her so she could see the page. "I used to have a tip jar when I worked the streets in New York and someone put this exact page in it one day."

"Why am I not surprised?" she said before taking a sip.

"I'm sure it's a coincidence."

She smirked. "Sure." Then another sip.

"I'm serious," he said. "It just showed up one day."

She nodded. "I bet it did."

Isa was playing with him, but Seba didn't care. He was too interested in the six-pointed star glyph. "This image actually helped me a lot. It basically maps out every social group and shows you the dynamics."

She tilted her head in interest. "Did you use it to assess the situation with me?"

"I mean … I guess. I don't really consciously think about it anymore, but you'd be the Alpha, holding the perimeters and conditions of your space."

"Right," she said with a nod.

"The guy who called you at the restaurant—"

"Robbie," she interjected.

"Robbie," he corrected, "would be a Beta, someone who stands in for you and sees your will done."

"Keep going."

"The two guys with him were Deltas, those who apply force to hold space and keep peace." He gestured at the yard, in general. "And pretty much everyone here are Gammas." He glanced at the band. "Well, except those guys. The guys in the band are Deltas who watch for Sigmas from the stage and signal you if they see trouble."

She smirked and finished off her bottle. "See? You don't even have to think about it. You're hardwired for this."

He shook his head and pointed to the bottom point of the star. "Not really. I've never understood Omegas."

She placed her bottle and studied him for a moment. "Interesting. What don't you understand?"

"What they are in the whole system," he said, tapping his finger on the definition. "I mean, '*The Omega holds the endgame*'? What's that supposed to mean? Who are they in a group like this? I've never found a reliable way to spot one."

"Ah," Isa said with a bit of a glint. "Well, first off, an Omega can be anyone—a child, a parent, an acquaintance, or a mate—but any healthy Alpha has one in their life."

Seba shook his head, rejecting the premise in reflex. "Well, I'm more of a lone wolf."

"And a lone wolf eventually becomes someone who thinks only of himself," she countered. "*No bueno.*"

Seba still bristled.

"I know," she teased. "I was like you once. When it was suggested that someone might be my anchor, all I could imagine was dead weight being slung over my shoulders."

Sounded about right.

"But I'm telling you, if an Alpha is like the earth—holding space for others to thrive—then an Omega is like the sun the Alpha circles so it doesn't become a cold, barren—and, yes—unanchored rock hurtling through space."

Well, when she put it like *that*.

"In my experience, the Omega holds the endgame because they give their Alpha a reason to hold steady and build something in this crazy world."

Seba fought the urge to look at Vic and studied the glyph in the book instead.

"Alphas, like us, see things as they are and calculate accordingly," Isa continued. "But without a vision or something to ground us, we can get lost in our power and start using it solely for our own benefit." Her eyes dropped in what seemed to be regret. "That's what I was doing when the Pimpernel found me ... proving how high I could go while bragging nothing could hold me down. I thought that was success. And I was going for it while leaving everyone else behind."

She was treading deep waters that weren't really Seba's

business to explore, but he had to ask. "What brought you back home?"

To his surprise, she smiled—her eyes lighting up with affection. "A wise mentor who helped me see some things, and an Omega who had been waiting for me all along."

Oh.

A softness came over Isa's face as she thought about the person Seba had a sneaking suspicion Isa wouldn't be naming for him. Not yet, anyway. He could sense Isa's protective streak under the love in her eyes.

When he saw that look, understanding started to sink in.

Isa's "Omega" was the one person she couldn't be objective about ... the one who made her all heart.

"So how do you spot one in a crowd?" he asked, knowing he was treading on tricky territory now that Isa was thinking of hers.

But Isa didn't seem to mind. "Well, they are both the strongest and most vulnerable in a group."

Seba shook his head. "That doesn't make sense."

That got a full smile. "It doesn't, does it? Not logically. But think of them like soil. Not only does everything they touch grow, but they're solid when you need to stand firm, and give way when it's time to dig in."

He chuckled. "Omegas are like dirt?"

She nodded, not laughing along. "Yes. And often treated like it if Alphas don't look out for them."

"Sounds like a one-sided relationship."

"It isn't," she said without hesitation. "Trust me, it's a symbiosis. The Alpha holds group space, and the Omega holds the Alpha. And, in that way, the Omega holds the endgame."

"Huh," Seba said, looking at the star again and trying to imagine the concept without thinking of a certain blonde.

Vic was his first thought when it came to everything Isa was saying. But he couldn't let the fact that his world currently revolved around keeping her alive confuse him into imagining she was something she wasn't.

Vic was many things, but she definitely wasn't dirt. Or soil. Or whatever. A star, definitely—and, by default, a sun he would gladly orbit, but they were from two different worlds and would separate soon.

It would be best if he avoided turning Isa's general statements into specific thoughts.

He closed the book in front him and looked up at Isa. "Thank you. For the book and your thoughts."

She nodded. "You're welcome. I hope you use them to make something of yourself."

He shrugged. "I'm not so bad at the moment."

Isa arched a brow. "Nah, if you're like I was, you're a self-serving loner with no purpose outside of profit."

Ouch. That pretty much hit home.

"So, if you want to thank me, find your sun and use all those skills you've got to grow something. Then you'll find out what life is all about."

"Okay, you can stop hammering that nail now," he said, holding up his hands in surrender. "I got it."

"Good. Because I'm sick of your girl glaring at me, so let's get you back where you belong."

His girl. Again, not technically true. But Seba didn't correct her.

Chapter 32

Vic and Seba ended up sleeping on the downstairs couches. The decision was not reached without a little controversy. All the teens had been mortified at the thought of a celebrity sleeping on the couch—one of the boys going so far as to estimate how many times he'd farted on it.

His mom responded that maybe it was time to start being nicer to the furniture.

A cacophony of Spanish had followed, as everyone pleaded their cases as to where Vic, in particular, should spend the night.

In the end, Seba made it clear they needed to be in the same room, but separate, and the couches offered a unique solution. Seba could push the one Vic slept on against the wall and position the second couch between hers and the entrance.

It was the only solution on the table where he could imagine getting any sleep and Vic had been fine with it, too. So sheets and blankets had been pulled out of closets and thirty minutes later, the house was quiet.

Laying on the undersized couch with a nightlight casting the room with a soft glow, Seba had to admit it had been a strange night. An awesome one. But strange.

He had a name for the blue flower now. A pimpernel. It was the seal of some do-gooder who was somehow connected to the book with pages that had been slipped into his tip jar more than a decade ago.

Weird stuff, but he felt a strange hum of excitement when he imagined it all might mean something.

He heard Vic's breathing even out behind his couch, and felt his own breathing start to slow and relax.

They were safe here. It was okay to sleep. They would be fine until morning.

His eyes started blinking shut, leaning in to the collective quiet when he saw someone sitting in the armchair in his peripheral vision.

His eyes flashed open and his head turned, ready to take them on … and saw nothing.

The chair was empty.

Odd.

He looked around, trying to find what might have cast a shadow that looked like a person. There was no plausible explanation. The only light came from behind the chair and what he'd thought he'd seen hadn't been a shadow. It had looked like a person sitting on a chair.

Seba turned his head back to its original position and tried to see the shape again.

Nothing.

On top of that, a gut-check confirmed they were safe.

It must have been the shape of closing eyelashes and a trick of light, he told himself when he was all out of other ideas.

Accepting they really were safe, Seba closed his eyes and got some rest.

Chapter 33

"Also," Vic said between huffing breaths as they hiked the next day. "Turns out, you're not the only conman here."

"Is that so?" Seba asked from in front of her, scanning the path as they went.

"It is," she announced. "Apparently, tons of people hate me because they buy the stuff I model and it *really* is absolute crap. Selina says she bought one of my bras for $40 once, and it didn't even last one wash!"

Vic was so good with names. Seba learned them and forgot them, as needed, but Vic remembered everyone she'd met the night before and already seemed to consider them friends.

Part of Seba admired that ability of hers. He should maybe try harder at things like that.

For the moment, however, he just kept the conversation going. "Wow. Even I'm not that bad. People get what they pay for with me."

She smacked his arm from behind. "Don't make me feel worse about it!"

"What?" he defended playfully as the trail widened and flattened out a little. "Even I don't go after kids' money."

When she moved up to walk next to him, her expression

was half-scowl, half-smile. Then the smile faded.

"I've gotta figure out a way to make it right, you know?" she huffed. "I mean … if we figure a way out of this, and all."

Seba had been putting a lot of thought into that.

The note from the Pimpernel asked him to watch her until 6:00 that night and it was 2:13. In less than four hours, the timer would run out, and Seba couldn't see what would change in that time.

Certainly not his commitment to keep her safe. He was on board to the end of the road on this. Whatever that looked like, he'd handle it, but the game would change when the clock struck 6:00 and Vic realized nothing was different.

They had to stop running at some point, and they needed a plan for that.

Feeling eyes on him, Seba looked up and spotted some hikers up ahead. "Incoming."

Vic looked up and spotted them—still a ways off—and tipped the brim of her hat down.

It was probably unnecessary at this point. No one had recognized her so far. The girls from last night had returned that morning with what they deemed an appropriate disguise for a Hollywood celebrity. A wig, an LA Galaxy cap, some aviator sunglasses, jean shorts, a shirt from a 5K run, and a pair of Chucks.

They'd taken over Vic's makeup, too, and by the time she had walked out of the bathroom Seba had to admit he wouldn't have recognized her on the street.

At six-foot-four and built like a double-wide at his shoulders, Seba turned out to be the harder one to disguise. But no one was really looking that hard at them out here on the trails. They all said hi and kept walking.

Seba was grateful for that. He had taken her out here to talk without interruptions, and it was time to get down to business.

"Have you thought about what you want to do when we

go back to the city?" he asked.

She bit her bottom lip as she thought about her answer and Seba looked away to keep his eyes on the group coming down the path. They didn't look like they were watching him back, but it felt like it.

"Yesterday, I didn't know," Vic confessed. "But last night was so awesome. I think it's the first party I've been to where people actually liked each other, and it made me realize I want that. I don't want to hide for the rest of my life and worry everyone I meet will sell me out, and maybe that means it's time to tell the truth and see what happens. I mean, if I tell everyone Evan is trying to kill me and then I die, at least he's a suspect, right?"

Her words were like a punch to his gut. "You're not dying."

"Right," she agreed. "I don't want to die either. But if I did—"

"You won't."

She pressed her lips together in doubt. "I might."

Seba stopped in his tracks. "You won't. Okay? Not on my watch."

She smiled under her aviators and he had to fight the urge to kiss her.

He started walking again. "I think telling the truth is a smart plan."

She caught up to him. "You do?"

"Yeah," he said as they came up on the other group. They were young, laughing, and into each other so they didn't look too hard.

"Hey," one of them said.

"Hey," Seba replied and then they were walking away from each other.

"So you think I should tell the truth," Vic said a few steps later.

"I think the only people who benefit from secrets are the guilty," he replied. "Privacy protects things that are personal, but secrets are about hiding shame. And I say it's past time for Evan Bauer to start coming face-to-face with his. I have a whole network who can make sure anything you want is posted everywhere overnight."

"Really?" She sounded giddy.

"Really," he agreed as a bug bit him on the neck.

He should have packed bug spray.

"So he wouldn't be able to track down who posted it and hu—ow!" She slapped at her neck. "I think a bug just bit me."

"Me, too," Seba said as the red flags of what just happened dropped in his mind.

He motioned for her to stand up, scanning the horizon for a reflection or a color out of place. Dizziness overtook him before he could make a full turn.

Vic seemed to notice.

"Hey, are you okay?" she asked, reaching up toward him.

Seba felt his vision narrowing as he looked down at her. "Vic, I screwed up. We're in trouble."

And he knew he was right when everything faded to black before he hit the ground.

Chapter 34

Great view, was Vic's first thought as her eyes blinked open. They immediately shut again thanks to a dull headache that seemed to stem from everywhere.

Her mouth felt dry. She needed water.

When she tried to sit up to go get some, Vic found she couldn't. That's when she noticed her ankles hurt, too. And her wrists. She squinted her eyes open to look at both.

Yeah … they probably hurt because they were strapped down.

Vic groaned—knowing they were in trouble. Again. Those had been the last words Seba had said to her, after all, and he had a knack for being right about things like that.

Last night, she'd been terrified at the restaurant—all those unsmiling faces staring at her like all they needed was a word and they'd riot. But Seba had been steady and said they were safe.

And he'd been right.

He'd also been right about them being safe at the hotel a block away from where her step-father attacked her.

Seba had been right about nearly everything since she'd met him. So if he said they were in trouble, the only thing left to do was figure out how much and what kind.

All Vic knew at the moment was that the sun was maybe an hour away from setting on the ocean and she was set up for a perfect view of it.

She recognized the view, but the room was new. Unable to see more than ivory carpet and floor-to-ceiling windows, Vic looked over her shoulder to see what else she could glean about her current situation.

The elegant room looked like an eighties rock band had their way with it. Empties lay strewn around the room and she was pretty sure she saw a line of coke ready to go on the coffee table.

The headache made it hard to look at anything too long, so Vic pinched her eyes shut, trying to push the pain away long enough to get a peek over her other shoulder.

When she spotted Seba—out cold and bound to a tabletop broken off its stand next to her—she didn't look any further. The tabletop looked to be fine marble and probably the only thing in the room their abductor trusted to hold Seba down.

Yes. They were definitely in trouble. Big trouble.

Maybe the worst kind of trouble.

Vic felt tears well in her eyes at the knowledge that she was the one who had gotten him into this situation. If it weren't for her crazy life, Seba would be somewhere else, doing just fine.

But he wasn't. Neither of them were. Vic was strapped to an unhinged door, Seba was bolted into marble, and nothing was fine.

Evan had found her somehow. Who knew how, but he'd found her like he always had and things were about to get bad again.

She should have seen this coming. It wasn't like things could end any other way. Evan Bauer always won. The best Vic could aim for now would be to figure out some reason for him to let Seba go. She deserved what was coming, but he didn't. He'd only been trying to help.

Seba didn't know the rules. Vic did, and she'd broken

them. The punishment should be hers alone.

She started working against her ropes on instinct, seeing if she could get them to give or find a weak spot somehow. All she succeeded in doing was making them tighter. She tried to rotate her wrist to get them to loosen again, but the damage was done. The knot was tied to slide and tighten when pulled on. Vic would need at least one free hand to loosen them.

When it came to saving the day, she was off to a great start.

Just then, a man walked past her to the massive window providing the gorgeous view. He had a ladder in one hand and a camera in the other.

He acted like she wasn't there, giving her plenty of time to look him over. He was maybe in his early forties and dressed like he spent a lot of time in Europe: pants just a shade too tight, gorgeous handmade boots that helped him get away with the pants, and a lightweight button-up shirt with one-too-many buttons undone.

Ignoring the fact he was being watched, the man eyeballed the distance between Vic and Seba before setting up the ladder and climbing. He seemed to check a monitor behind Vic as he positioned the camera before removing an adhesive strip and connecting the camera to the wall above the window. Then he climbed down the ladder and folded it up again.

Vic didn't stoop so low as to ask him what he was doing. That was obvious. He would either be recording or broadcasting what came next. Or both. That part didn't confuse her. Nor did the cold, flat affect of his eyes. She knew such eyes well, even when they smiled and acted like the life of the party.

What confused her was his arguably handsome face and the fact she hadn't seen it before.

"Who are you?" she asked.

The man kept working like he hadn't heard her.

Classic.

"Look," she said. "I'm not going to start losing it because you pretend I'm not here. I'm genuinely curious. I thought I knew all of my step-father's men, but you're new."

He disappeared behind her again, his footsteps eerily silent as he moved back into her blind spot.

"You know you want to monologue," she called after him. "Don't think I don't know your type. You're all narcissists who love to brag about how smart you are, how dumb I am, and how that gives you the right to do what you do. So you might as well get started. It's not like I'm going anywhere."

Silence.

Silver lining: her headache had mostly disappeared, so that was nice. Adrenaline was good for something.

Vic looked Seba's way and found him still out cold.

"C'mon, tell me!" she called out. "What was the stupidest thing I did that helped you catch me? What made you want to hit your own head and tell yourself someone as stupid as me has it coming?"

The man reappeared and stood over her, smiling. Then he looked over at Seba.

"When you trusted him," he said before disappearing again.

The reply hit her like a slap and she started to panic at what exactly he meant by that until it dawned on her that panicking was exactly what he wanted her to do.

So she settled herself down.

"I know, right?" she called after him. "This guy shows up out of nowhere, and I just *follow* him? Who does that?"

"It is inexplicable," he said from behind her.

No. It wasn't. Now that Vic was lying strapped to a door, she knew exactly why she had followed Seba so quickly. His eyes. She hadn't pegged it at the time, but there was something very honest in the supposed conman's eyes. He cared about her out of the gate and that's why she'd followed him.

But her captor would never understand something like that. He had cold snake eyes. Anyone who trusted him wasn't looking at his eyes. They were looking somewhere else.

That was the difference.

Seba was genuine and this guy was psycho, and nothing the psycho said would take that shred of sanity away from her.

She needed it if they had any shot of getting out of this.

"I always wonder," she mused out loud. "Why do guys like you work so hard to impress my step-father? I've wondered that my entire life. I mean, he's just a guy. There's really nothing all that impressive about him, outside of his bank account. Yet he has line after line of men like you ready to line up and kneel for him."

"Watch it, missy," the man said from a different location behind her. "You're not in a position to annoy me."

"Uh, yeah. I am," she countered. "Unless you want to let us go. I'll go take my observations somewhere else."

He chuckled, the sound once again coming from a new location. He was playing with her.

"I have to be honest," he said. "I didn't expect you to be this lippy."

"Well, unfortunately for you, your tactics aren't all that original. It's been at least eight years since this little setup has gotten the desired reaction from me."

A moment of silence, then, "Are you trying to piss me off?"

"Are you capable of any other emotion?" she countered. "Anger and fantasies of overpowering others is kind of your wheelhouse, right? Or are you a different kind of crazy?"

No answer.

He was mad. That was progress.

The man clearly had a premeditated plan, but now he was mad and trying to control his impulses. She could feel it. Guys like Tight Pants could only feign control for short amounts of time before bowing to their impulses.

If Vic could get him off script, that would be a win.

"So what's your favorite thing about my step-father?" she asked. "Be honest. Is it the amenities? The money? Or do you feel a personal bond?"

"For your information," he said, tone tight, "I've never met your step-father and I have no intention to. I'm not here for him. I'm here for me."

Oh.

She felt a chill run up her spine.

Point: Psycho.

He'd clearly shared the information to put her off her game. And it worked. Vic suddenly felt quite adrift.

If Evan wasn't calling the shots on this, maybe she really didn't know what was going on.

"So you work a day job and abduct people on weekends for funsies?" she asked.

"Call it a hobby," he said, sounding smug again. He was back in control. Back on plan.

Vic looked over at Seba. He was still out—his chest barely rising and falling as he took shallow, slow breaths. But he was alive. Maybe he'd wake up or maybe he'd stay out. There was no way of guessing what this guy was thinking of doing, only what he wanted out of it.

And Vic wouldn't be playing along.

"I'd ask if your mom didn't love you enough," she sighed, "but we both know she did. We both know you were a spoiled child with parents who tried to love you through the fact that you're a terrible person, while you told yourself that they were stupid for not seeing you for what you are."

No answer.

"You have no idea how many parents of psychos I've met at parties," she continued. "Normal people—nice people— who pinch their little psycho's cheeks and tell them they're good kids who work too hard. I bet your parents are nice."

Suddenly, he was in her face. "You don't know anything

about my parents so you'd better shut your mouth!"

She rolled her eyes, making sure he saw it. "Right. In your version of events, they're terrible and neglectful, right? And it's all their fault you like to hurt things, but seriously, aren't you sick of blaming them? Don't you think there should be a point where we grow up and stop blaming our parents for our actions?"

His jaw clenched.

"What do you think a good age for that would be? Eighteen? Or is that too young?"

His eyes narrowed.

"Or twenty-four, like me?" she offered. "Maybe take the whole year to go through all our baggage so we can start our second quarter-century on a new leaf?"

"You should stop talking." His breath smelled like caviar and crackers with a hint of wine. Well, at least he wasn't starving. He could have hungry breath. Or coffee breath.

Silver lining.

"How about forty?" she asked, ignoring him.

And just like that, he was mad again. A vein raised on his temple, then he disappeared behind her again.

"I bet your mom makes a nice Sunday dinner," she called after him.

He was back, caviar breath and all. "You're lucky I have a plan I'm following or I'd be doing something very different right now."

"I know," she said, doing her best to sound bored as her hands started tingling from loss of blood flow. "But you're not the boss here, are you? I mean, this is your hobby and all, but those cameras tell me you like being watched. You need the reactions and reputation to give yourself meaning."

When he blinked in surprise, she knew she had him.

"It's not enough to just do your hobby anymore, is it?" she taunted. "You need people to watch and be shocked to feel a thrill anymore, am I right?"

He glared.

She shrugged. "Let's just agree that I'm right."

The ring of his slap echoed long after he had disappeared behind her again. Vic worked her jaw, making sure it was still in place before smiling to herself.

He might untie her yet.

Next to her, Seba stirred. The slap seemed to have roused him because he turned his head to look right at her before his eyes opened for a beat and squinted closed again.

He probably had a headache like she had.

"Hey," she said softly, her heart giving a strange little lurch when his eyes blinked up for her. Man, he was beautiful.

"What's happening?" he muttered right before his arms flexed against his bindings. Muscles and veins grew with the strain and the metal actually groaned a little.

Mr. Tight Pants was *so* lucky he'd bolted Seba down. It was the only way a loser like him could win.

"You were right," Vic said softly. "We're in trouble."

Seba's eyes blinked open and he looked her dead in the eye to get a sense of how serious she was being before testing all four bindings with all he had. Nothing even came close to budging.

"Ah, you're both awake," the guy said, coming around to stand between them. He looked at Seba. "You know, I thought she was going to be the easier one to break, but now that we're all in the same room, I'm pretty sure you're the one who needs to go last."

Seba tried a new angle as he pulled. "What's going on? Who are you?"

"Allow me to introduce myself," Tight Pants said with a smile. "I'm Finder 0-1-1."

Chapter 35

Seba could have screamed. He nearly did as he gave the metal clamps all he could as they bit in and punished him for his efforts.

Finder011? The man who had been helping Seba for nearly a year? Building trust? The man who had helped Seba find Vic that first night and secured the yacht for them yesterday?

Seba had been so careful to make sure Vic wasn't being tracked, only to be the one to tell the one hunting them where they were at every pace?

He'd actually *thanked* the guy for his help yesterday.

This time Seba did scream, flexing against the bindings, not to get free this time, but giving his frustration somewhere to go.

"Yep," he heard Finder011 say. "You're definitely going last."

Then the man walked off.

"Hey, look at me," Vic whispered.

He couldn't.

He couldn't look Vic in the eye knowing that he'd led the danger right to them.

"Seba."

He shook his head, still not looking at her. "I'm so sorry."

"You know who he is?"

Seba nodded, hating that when he tried to blink back his tears of frustration they had nowhere to go but out the sides of his eyes and down his temples. He couldn't even wipe them away.

He felt like an idiot.

"Seba?"

Why did she keep saying his name like that? Like this wasn't all his fault.

Right then, The Finder came back with a portable screen and set it up under a camera Seba spotted for the first time over the window.

"Hey!" Vic objected as the screen rose to its full height to block the window. "That was just getting pretty."

What was she thinking? Did she not see how serious this situation was?

"Don't worry," The Finder said. "I'm going to give you a better show."

"Better than the sun?" she countered. "Well, someone is full of himself."

Was Vic high? What was going on? What had Seba missed?

All those questions disappeared when he watched the man walk up to Vic and lean in close enough to kiss her. "Don't worry, baby. I'm going to answer so many questions for you tonight. You're actually going to thank me."

Seba nearly blacked out in rage at the urge to punch the man and his inability to do so.

"Don't touch her!" he yelled out instead, earning an amused smile for his effort.

"No?" the man said, as his hand dipped down to Vic's waist and made contact. "Touch."

In that moment, Seba realized what the man was doing and that Seba was making things worse for Vic by letting it work. He had to dial back. Calm down. Shut up.

He needed to shut down his emotions and start playing smart. He knew that.

So why couldn't he do it?

The Finder straightened and smiled. "You know, I'm not surprised often, but I really expected the two of you to be playing opposite roles at this point. I like the change, though … I'll take it."

He then walked over to the windows and started pulling the blackout curtains closed. The room dimmed with each closed curtain, but didn't go full dark.

"Seba, look at me," Vic said.

He felt like crying when he heard the kindness in her voice. They were probably about to die and Seba had been the one to lead the killer right to them. She had no business being nice right now.

But he owed it to her to look if she asked.

He turned his head, nearly cracking at the gentleness he found in her blue eyes. "I'm so sorry, Vic."

She shook her head. "I'm the target here. I'm sorry you got dragged into all this."

"Oh, it's 100% your fault he's here, Vic," The Finder interjected as he closed the final curtain. "Your step-mother saw how dreamy you got after kissing him a few years back. She was the one who guessed he would make the most believable partner in this crime."

Vic jerked in surprise, the news clearly getting to her. This seemed to please The Finder because he walked over to crouch next to her and kept talking.

"The backup plan was to have a fan do a whole murder-suicide thing." He scrunched his nose in distaste. "It would have worked, but I like the poetry of this better. You'll go out like your parents and people believe an echo like that so much quicker. Everyone knows the apple never falls far from the tree, and it makes for such a better picture."

His words seemed to stun Vic. She stared at him—mouth half-open as the man reached out and booped her nose with his finger.

"There you are," he said playfully. "I was worried you might not come out and play."

Then he walked behind them and turned on a projector.

"Vic?" Seba called.

This time she was the one who didn't want to look at him.

"Are you okay?"

She didn't say anything, but he saw her shake her head in the dim light. Then a projector turned on behind them and a video appeared on the white screen showing an ornate room filled with formally dressed people sitting in chairs.

Standing in front of them on a stage, a man in a tux stood with a sculpted bust on display next to him. He was talking and pointing, but there was no audio so Seba wasn't sure what was happening.

"What is this?" he called out.

"The auction for my portrait of your lives," The Finder replied.

Chapter 36

"Of course, my step-mom is there," Seba heard Vic say, her tone bitter as she watched the screen. "How did I not see this coming?"

"No clue," The Finder replied helpfully. "You must have sensed how much she hated you all this time."

"Yeah," Vic agreed without hesitation. "But she always stayed away."

"Right," The Finder agreed. "But you know what she couldn't get away from? Your shadow on her daughter. Do you know how crazy that drives a mother? To have everyone talking about the hated step-child and never the golden child? At least Evan saw you as an income stream. He was your protection throughout the years. He liked the money you brought in and the clout he got with his peers. But all Miriam got was '*Marsha! Marsha! Marsha!*' from her sad little Jan, and it eventually drove her to me. I don't take many cases, mind you, but yours was special. A lot of people who have caused me trouble in the past are laying bets on you for some reason, and I was in the mood to make them all eat crow. So here we are. Tada. You're all caught up."

Vic had no response and neither did Seba, honestly. It was a lot to process.

"Huh," The Finder added after a beat. "I guess you were right. I did want to monologue. Smart girl."

Seba didn't get the reference but Vic seemed to. She watched the screen, eyes shimmering, and Seba was overcome with the need to find a way out of the clasps. He started twisting and pulling as The Finder kept talking.

"And since you're listening so nicely, I'll give you a spoiler about the painting I did for you. I named it *Apples and Trees* and it's up next. You'll see it, and you'll see why this scenario is so much better with a lover at your side rather than a crazed stalker fan. But Seba was so uncooperative about running into you for so long, I thought he was going to be a no-show and we'd have to play the whole angle of a fan wanting to die with you like your parents died. Much less ideal. Cliché in the bad way."

Seba could wedge his right hand about 60% out, but it wasn't nearly enough so he started testing the balance of the table itself.

"We've been planting stories about your party-girl habits for weeks," The Finder continued. "So you can imagine my joy when you—of your own volition— run off with a conman who beats up your guards on the way out. I mean … talk about making it clear you died while away from the Bauer's protection. Because they'll, of course, say they tried to save you. But you were uncontrollable and addicted, just like your parents. They'll frown and sigh in interviews saying, no matter how much they gave you, you were driven to follow in your parents' cursed footsteps."

Vic's voice was cold when she replied. "Everyone knows I don't touch drugs because of my parents."

"Well, people remember what they want to remember," The Finder said with indifference. "Memories tend to be very suggestible."

Vic didn't argue the point, and Seba was having no luck moving the marble slab. It was solidly in position, not giving an inch.

On the screen, two men walked in and started to remove the bust from the stage.

"Ah, here we are," The Finder said. "The grand finale. Are you ready to find out how much your lives are going to earn me?"

He turned up the audio and stepped out of sight just as a draped picture was carried onto the stage.

"And now, for our final item," the auctioneer said on the screen. *"I am told we will have a remote feed joining us. Is it ready?"*

The Finder walked to stand between them again, only this time he was wearing a mask. On the screen, Seba saw a feed of them appear on the stage—he and Vic strapped down, The Finder standing between them with his face hidden.

"Yes," The Finder said. "We are ready."

Seba wanted to scream, but was certain that's what The Finder wanted him to do.

Resignation setting in, he turned to look at Vic and found her already watching him.

"Excellent," the auctioneer said. *"Would you like to introduce yourself?"*

"I am Ceravene, the artist." The Finder said. "With me, are the subjects of my piece, Vic Davalos and Sebastian Kahn."

There was so much to be said and no time to say it as Seba locked eyes with Vic.

"Thank you for the introduction," the auctioneer said. *"Now, for our final item up for auction this evening, we have a rare treat: an original piece, hand signed by the artist, entitled, Ceravene: Portrait of a Starbreaker."*

The Finder grew statue-still as the cloth was pulled off the picture, revealing the spitting image of Finder011 looking into a mirror. On one side of the mirror, the man reaching out with a friendly handshake. On the other, he was stabbing forward with a knife.

The Finder ran up to the screen—getting as close as he

could to the picture. Shock etched into every part of his body as the auctioneer said, *"This piece comes with the man, himself. Ceravene will be delivered to the highest bidder, along with his portrait. I will start the bidding at one dollar."*

"No!" Ceravene breathed before spinning to run for the door.

He made it one step before his chest seemed to run into an invisible bar. His body folded in half, mid-air, before flying back and landing short of the screen.

A hooded figure stepped out of nowhere. A woman.

"Hi," she said, wiggling her fingers to The Finder in greeting as she moved to stand over him.

"Can I get one dollar?" the auctioneer said on the screen.

People in the onscreen audience seemed to be panicking as The Finder made an attempt to make it past the hooded woman.

This time the woman took both legs out from under her with a simple trip. As he fell, one hand reached out to pull off his mask as the other planted into the base of his neck and slammed him face-first into the carpet.

Part of Seba purred when the man didn't rebound right away. The girl might be the size of a gymnast but she did good work.

"Fifty cents," the auctioneer said on the screen. *"Can I get fifty cents for the life of Ceravene, the first Starbreaker to be captured in three hundred years."*

Everyone on the screen was trying to get out of the room, but the doors were locked and a row of guards now stood in front of the auctioneer.

In front of Seba, the woman already had The Finder hogtied. She whispered, "Thanks for teaching me how to catch Starbreakers. I think I'll do it again sometime," into his ear before leaving him to struggle against his ties so she could head over to untie Vic.

"Hold tight," she said to Seba as she passed. "We'll get to you."

We?

"A penny?" the auctioneer said, but the room wasn't listening to him anymore. They were climbing over each other and trying to battle ram the doors.

It was then Seba realized he couldn't see the hooded woman in the feed showing their location. It looked like Vic was freeing herself. Seba looked from the woman to the screen and back again.

How could she be visible in one spot and not the other?

The question took a back seat to the fact that she'd gotten both of Vic's hands free and started rubbing them like she was trying to get blood into them. Vic grimaced like it hurt while staring up at the woman like she couldn't believe what she was seeing.

"I'm sorry," Seba heard the hooded woman said softly to Vic. "We had to wait until he confirmed his identity on the broadcast to make a move."

On the screen, the auctioneer changed tones.

"Very well," he declared. *"I will open the bidding up to our remote audience tonight. Ceravene is no longer included. Bids will be for the portrait only, hand signed with the seal of the Cobalt Pimpernel. The discerning eye will notice a nuanced addition to the flower in the form of a casted shadow, or Shade. Please note, all funds will be directed to the Cobalt Pimpernel's coffers to be used as he sees fit. I will start the bidding at $1 million dollars. Do I have—I have $50 million from the Second Son. Do I hear 51?"*

A man who looked weirdly like an actor Seba might have seen on a big screen squatted down next to him and started running a sparking blade under the bolts pinning Seba down to get him free.

"Hold still until I get both your hands and legs free," the man commanded.

Seba did as instructed, eager to get free. He checked on Vic to see how she was handling the surreal change of events and found her smiling at him in disbelief.

Are you okay? she mouthed to him.

He nodded as his left leg was freed. "You?"

A tear slipped from her eye as she nodded, the hooded woman still massaging circulation into her hands.

Seba really needed this dude to hurry up so he could get to her.

"I've got $65 million, from the young prince," the auctioneer said on the screen. *"Do I hear 66?"*

Seba's right leg was free.

Everything ached, but Seba didn't care at the moment. All he wanted was for his last arm to get free so he could get off the marble slab and check on Vic himself. His body was starting to shake with shock and he was pretty sure he wouldn't feel right until he could feel for himself that Vic was okay.

It was clear she was currently in good hands, but Seba could imagine better ones.

The last clamp came free with a light pinch and Seba started to stand only to realize his feet had fallen asleep while bound. Pins and needles shot through his legs as he tried to stand, forcing him to take a moment to stomp some life back into them.

As he did, the man walked over to The Finder, pressed a device to the base of his neck and pulled a trigger. He cried out, but didn't seem to be harmed.

Then the man who had freed Seba freed The Finder, too, who didn't waste a beat to dart for the door.

The liberator made no move to chase him.

Pain forgotten, Seba surged to his feet and started after him. "After all that, you're going to let him go?"

The man stopped him with one hand—a dead stop, with no give to it at all. Seba froze in a moment of pure shock as he sensed the other man's raw power.

The man held up a cell phone, showing Seba a profile on it labeled: Ceravene.

"This just went out to people around the world," the man

said. "His identity is known. His associates and deeds are also known. His location is forever known. Anyone who assists him from here on out will also be known. He is marked with more enemies in this world than you can imagine. So you may pursue him, if you wish. But ask yourself if that's really where you want to be right now."

Then he sent a pointed look toward Vic.

Chapter 37

"Looks like your man is ready to take over," the girl in the hood said with a knowing smirk.

Even in the dim light, the woman had the most striking eyes. They were like vivid blue stars with pupils, which was about as surreal as everything else about her—including her jacket. The fabric felt like some blend that landed between silk and velvet, but it seemed a little too trite to ask her about it right then.

Her rescuer's hands worked their way up from Vic's hand to her elbow in fluid motions, urging circulation into the hands Vic thought might be headed for amputation. Now they were starting to look the right color again.

When the woman switched to her other hand and repeated the motion, Vic felt a ping of recognition when the woman's grip reached her forearm.

In reflex, Vic pinned her free hand over the woman's.

"You," she breathed. "You were the one who caught me on the building."

The woman winked then finished her way up to Vic's elbow.

"Thank you!" Vic said as she pinned her hands again.

The woman seemed regretful. "Are you kidding? I

wanted to save you long before you fell, but that was the only way to get you safely to Seba." She bit her lip. "You might want to thank me now, but you'll probably hate me later when you realize all the things I didn't stop. And I'm sorry for that. But to catch this guy, we couldn't tip him off. We had to walk him into his own trap by letting things play out naturally. I was only allowed to step in when lives were on the line."

Vic looked her in the eye. "I will never hate you. I might get a tattoo of your hand holding on to my forearm, but I'll never hate you."

The woman grimaced. "I'd pass on that tattoo, but I'm glad we're good."

Good? She was glad they were *good*?

Was she kidding?

Vic was ready to name her firstborn after this woman— male or female.

The woman tilted her head over to where the men were arguing. "The guy with me is here to escort you to someplace safe where you'll be able to sort things out. I'm pretty sure the other guy over there wants to hold your hand while you go there, but that's your call."

What started out as blush at the mention of Seba turned to disappointment. "You're not coming with me?"

The woman shook her head. "No. My day isn't done. I've gotta go, but Ren's going to take you somewhere and help you set everything right, okay?"

Vic nodded. "So this is it?"

The woman smiled. "Probably. But I'm cheering for you. You're going to do amazing things in this world. I can feel it, so I'll be watching."

Vic was too flattered to make a reply as the woman gave her a light pat and headed for the door without another word.

A man waited for her there, wearing a sharp suit. He was average height and average build with a standard haircut Vic saw on half the businessmen she knew. He waited for the hooded woman to reach him, then joined her pace before they both walked out the door.

Gone. Just like that.

On the other side of her, someone pulled a curtain open, letting in the sunset. She heard Seba say her name and spotted him in reflex. Then they both reached out and met each other halfway.

Chapter 38

Jack walked down the hall of the downtown skyscraper—employees racing past him in the opposite direction. He let them go as he followed the hallway to large, mahogany doors marking the entrance to the boss's domain.

The secretary's desk stood empty, everything still on it as if she was on a break. But she was gone, as were the two men who usually stood on either side of the door as security.

Jack pushed the mahogany doors open, leaving them open wide behind him as he stepped into the office.

The boss sat at his desk, mouth curved down into an angry frown at something he saw on his screen. When he heard Jack, he looked up.

"Who are you?" he snapped. "How did you get in here?"

"Hello, Mr. Bauer," Jack said, holding out his business card. "I'm here to advise you of your situation."

The man laughed, reaching for the button to signal his secretary. "My situation is whatever I want it to be."

Right then, Evan's cell phone rang.

"That call is from your wife," Jack said, taking a seat across from Bauer. "You can call her back later. Everything she has to say to you will make more sense after you talk to me."

Evan all but snarled as he pressed the button for his secretary. "Evelyn, get security in here. Then fire yourself."

Dead air answered Evan on the intercom while his cell phone kept ringing in the pocket.

"Evelyn!"

"No one is coming to help you," Jack said when it was clear Evan's secretary would not be replying. "Like I said, I'm here to discuss your situation. Civilly, if possible. But trust me when I say, I have someone with me who doesn't mind if you want to make things uncivil. Your choice."

Jack watched as Evan's reply came in the form of reaching toward the drawer where he stored his gun. He jerked the drawer open and reached in, only to have the drawer slam shut on his hand.

The billionaire hissed in pain, cradling the damaged hand in his other with a look of shock on his face. "I think it's broken!"

"Like I said," Jack replied, leaning back in the chair as Evan's cell phone gave its final ring. "Civil or uncivil. Your choice. But today is your day of reckoning and we will be starting with your ledgers."

Chapter 39

From the torn-up high-rise in Los Angeles, Vic and Seba had been escorted to a jet at a private airport and flown to some type of villa under the cover of night. The flight had been short so Vic was pretty sure they were still in California. Somewhere. It felt like a different country, though.

They'd seen it first by torchlight—insanely romantic as stars shone bright in the moonless sky—then again by morning's light.

The architecture of the compound was unreal. The only time Vic had seen anything like it had been in storybooks—everything circular and arched with pristine gardens and flowing streams and lakes.

Everything Vic saw was more unreal than the last. One of the hilltop buildings had a freaking waterfall of fire that somehow circulated like regular water. Pools of actual water reflected like mirrors—bridges built over them to create perfect geometric images when viewed from the shores.

When she'd seen one that made a perfect reflected circle, with jewels reflecting both under the bridge and in the pool, she turned to Seba and asked, "Can you forge that?"

He'd studied the perfection, and nodded. "For you? Yes."

She'd nearly tripped and they hadn't even been walking.

It all felt like a dream.

For the most part, Seba took it all in silence—his expressions as taken aback as she felt.

Ren had told them they had free range to go anywhere but the main building. He'd said Vic's presence would be requested there later, but to enjoy the amenities in the meantime.

She hadn't even asked about amenities. She'd just tried to see everything there was to see as she took mental notes of how amazing architecture could be.

It made her want to learn how to design structures, too, not just clothes.

The other thing she took note of was the security. For the first time, Vic thought she might understand the whole vibe the guards around Buckingham Palace were going for. The men—and some women—on the property stood as still as statues as they kept their posts.

Utter stillness, like they were meditating and radiantly aware at the same time. But it was a weird kind of radiance that made them disappear and blend into everything around them like they were a part of it. Like a rock or a flower. Easy to notice, easy to ignore, but definitely fully aware of her.

It was both inspiring and unsettling.

"So…" she said to Seba when they were about twenty steps past the closest guard. "You said my guards sucked. I'm guessing these guys are the real deal, right?"

He nodded, his hand tightening on hers slightly. Vic loved it when he did that without thinking about it.

"These guys are next-level," he said. "I've never seen anything like them. Anywhere."

He didn't sound happy about it. He sounded like a man who didn't want to be replaced, and Vic fought a smile.

Every signal he sent that he didn't want to let go filled her with hope that maybe she might come out of all of this with something besides nightmares.

They should probably talk about that. It just never seemed to be a good time. Every time they caught a beat to rest, it seemed like a new curveball came sailing their way.

"Who's that?" he breathed in a tone that had Vic glancing around territorially. When she spotted who Seba was asking about, Vic got a little breathy, too.

"I have no idea."

Why were all the women they kept running into so beautiful?

First, there was Isa, with her full lips and Latin curves. Then there was the girl in the hood with eyes like stars. And now, a statuesque goddess was walking their way like elegance in motion.

With a decade under her belt of working runways, Vic knew a thing or two about walking. And a master class was strutting her way.

Tall and lithe, the woman walked like she expected the world to move for her, and Vic had no doubt that the world actually did.

And the suit she was wearing?

Divine.

The only thing Vic didn't like about it was that she hadn't designed it.

Vic gaped until she realized she wasn't the only one spellbound. Next to her, Seba looked like he was seeing the Red Sea part.

"Hey," she said, giving his arm a slap fueled with more than a little jealousy. "You're staring."

"You are, too," he whispered back, still watching. "Who are these people?"

"We are the mediators in separating the Davalos estate from the Bauer's," the woman replied in a full voice, covering the remaining distance as she spoke. When she reached them, she held out her hand to shake each of theirs, saying their names in turn. "Victoria. Sebastian. It's good to finally meet. My name is Margot Harbour, and you can think of me as the lawyer assigned to Victoria's case."

Whoa. Seriously? This was a lawyer's house?

Vic looked around again. "I don't think I can afford you."

Margot laughed, dark brown eyes glinting with amusement as she regarded Vic with what looked like respect. "Don't worry. The Bauers are paying in this situation. Trust me. You will see no commissions or fees for my services."

That seemed way too good to be true. Everything about Margot did. Her towering heels were handmade, and the suit ... up close, it was hard not to touch it or ask to see its stitching.

"I— this is probably the wrong thing to say right now— but I love your suit!" Vic gushed, feeling like an inarticulate fangirl for the first time in her life.

"Thank you," Margot said with a gracious smile. "I'm actually a fan of your designs, so I figured it was a fitting choice for our meeting."

Vic felt like she might stroke out at the news. Instead, she managed a graceless, "Well, you look stunning."

"Again, thank you," Margot replied with a light tilt of acknowledgment before turning to face Seba. "Unfortunately, I'm afraid we've reached the part where you and Victoria go separate ways, Sebastian."

Seba's hand tightened on hers possessively and Vic's heart picked up its pace in a giddy response.

"I don't think so," he said.

"I'm afraid it's non-negotiable on your part," Margot said calmly. "We brought you here together so you could know the other is safe while we came to terms with the Bauers. That's done now, which means it's now time for Victoria to make some decisions."

"I can wait for her here," Seba said firmly.

When Margot shook her head, her dark eyes chilled. "No. You will wait in Los Angeles. And she will find you when she is ready."

Whoa. Words came out of the woman's mouth like edicts. One thing was certain: Vic never wanted to be opposite this woman in an actual courtroom.

"Why can't I stay?" Seba had the nerve to ask. Vic sure wouldn't have had the guts.

Margot's gaze was cool, but not unkind. "Considering that a man has been making all of Victoria's decisions for the past twelve years, I don't think another man influencing her now is what she needs. Victoria has to choose what she wants, for her own reasons. Which means it's time for you to go wait in Los Angeles."

Seba's thumb rubbed across the back of Vic's hand, and Vic had a sense the soothing gesture was more for him than for her.

Vic turned to face him "It's okay. I'll be okay."

"I know," he said, doing that thing where it looked like he wanted to kiss her. He'd been doing it a lot over the past 24 hours, but he never made the move. Vic knew she could be the one to lean in, but she kind of wanted him to do it.

They'd kissed once before and Vic had been the one to pull him in. It was his turn.

So why wasn't he making the move? She was right there.

"I'll give you two privacy to say your goodbyes," Margot said, but Seba seemed to surprise them both when he simply pulled Vic into a solid hug before stepping away.

"Do what you've got to do," he said, his eyes seeming to burn with something unsaid.

Whatever it was, Vic really wanted him to say it.

One of his thumbs moved along her cheek as he seemed to study her face like he wasn't sure if he would see it again. "You need to look at everything and decide what's next for you." He took a step away. "Come find me when you know, okay?"

Vic didn't want him to go. At all.

Her whole world was about to shift, and part of her *wanted* him to tell her what to do when she stepped into the room with the lawyer.

But her lawyer was right. That was the exact reason he shouldn't be there.

Vic had to do this part on her own, and part of her loved Seba a little more for helping her accept that.

"See you in L.A.," she replied, giving him the kiss he deserved in her mind as she sent him a smile.

Based on how he swallowed, he got the subliminal message. "I'll be waiting."

Then they were escorted off in separate directions.

Chapter 40

Standing on the observation side of a one-way mirror, Jack allowed himself a satisfied smile as Margot and Vic got down to business.

Few things were more gratifying in Jack's line of work than watching the innocent get what they had coming. After being robbed their whole lives, few understood what the truth held for them on a day of reckoning.

Especially when Margot was splitting the bill.

The woman was forever fair in her divisions, but ice cold.

"So this is why Margot couldn't help us on the case," Kali deduced from next to him.

Jack nodded. "Royals can play ball when others on the board range from Fours to Eights. But since there is no other system on the earth that can handle Twos, Threes, Nines, and Tens, the Royals act as judges and mediators in that realm, while we non-Royals act as police. The Royals can't walk around devastating everyone they find problematic. That's tyranny. So they wait for someone to bring in lawbreakers and ask for their case to be heard. Only then do the Royals step in."

Kali nodded as if that made sense. "And since Miriam Bauer hired Ceravene, the Bauers get the Royal treatment."

Jack nodded, no longer surprised by how quickly she caught on. "Exactly."

She tapped her finger against her temple playfully. "I'm getting it. Your world here might be weird, but it does make a strange level of sense."

His world?

Jack decided to leave it alone.

"So does helping catch a Starbreaker mean you're allowed to tell me what card they are in the infamous deck?"

"Yes," Jack replied. "But it's tradition for the apprentice to at least guess first."

"Three of Spades," she said without hesitation.

Jack's eyebrows popped. "Mind showing your work on that one?"

"I have a theory about the number system," she said, talking with her hands to demonstrate. "Sixes are the center point, but it seems all the numbers going out from there are mirrors of each other. Fives are the inverses of Sevens, Fours of Eights, and so on."

"Go on," Jack prompted.

"To generalize types, Sevens seem willing to live or die for a belief, Eights are people who are loyal to the Royals, Nines—like Wanda—are loyal only to their own mind, and Tens—like Tiki—track a single truth. Reflect that the opposite way, and a killer with no loyalties or personal vision would be a Three."

Jack had heard the numbers described many ways before, but never like that. "And why do you think Starbreakers are Spades?"

"They are a master of frames," she replied, as if it was that simple. "Frames are like a lens, and Spades are the master of lenses."

Unreal. Her work checked out. It made him feel like a proud parent in a way.

"Am I right?" she asked.

"You are correct."

She looked pleased as he returned his attention to Vic on the other side of the mirror.

"I knew it," she said as Vic gasped.

"My parents' estate is worth how *much?"*

Jack turned volume up on the speakers a bit.

"Just over $257 million," came Margot's reply over the speakers. *"That is separate from the 70% Bauer has been gleaning since the beginning of your career."*

Vic looked shell shocked. *"Does that include Nora's 15%?"*

"No," Margot replied. *"To date, you have only received 15% of your monetization, so we will be rectifying that, as well, in a restitution amounting to $153.7 million."*

Vic leaned back in her seat, visibly stunned.

"I'm also pleased to inform you that we were able to reclaim this for you from your parents' estate," Margot said, sliding a jewelry box across the table.

Vic flipped the velvet box open and her face brightened. *"My mom's necklace. You found it!"*

"It was actually never lost," Margot replied, her tone soft. *"I'm told the one you were wearing before was a replica that was used as a tracking device."*

Vic was silent for a moment, then she started to laugh. *"Of course, it was. You know, that doesn't even surprise me. I think part of me actually knew,"* she said, pulling the necklace out of the box and undoing the clasp. *"I just couldn't say anything because, you know, I was the crazy one in that house. Ask anyone."*

Then she put the necklace on.

"You are an incredibly strong woman, Victoria," Margot said, and Jack could feel the respect wafting off of her.

Margot genuinely liked Victoria Davalos.

"Thanks," Vic said with a bit of a laugh in her voice. *"Kind of a survival requirement at this point, if you know what I mean."*

"I do," Margot said with a slight nod.

"Whoa," Kali said from next to him. "Look at Margot keeping it real."

Jack was as surprised as Kali.

"Yeah?" Vic said, looking a bit hesitant but hopeful that she might actually be talking to someone who understood.

Margot nodded in reply.

"How do you handle it?" Vic asked shyly and, next to Jack, Kali actually leaned forward to listen to the answer.

Margot was eternally frosty with Kali. The two rarely spoke. But Kali never seemed to return Margot's cold sentiments. If anything, they only made Kali pay more attention.

"I find it helpful not to think of the past as who I am, but as experiences I can access and use however I want," Margot replied. *"Experience can be wisdom, if we let it be. Or it can be an eternal wound for the same reason."*

She took a breath, as if debating whether to go on, then went for it.

"The Bauers, and many around them, taught you terrible things about what humans are capable of. People like them can win if we're so busy looking back that we forget to move forward. No one can build a heaven without understanding the gradients of hell. So those who have seen hell have a choice to make between whether to replicate what they've known, or banish it for something better. The choice is always ours."

Vic was silent for several moments, looking at the necklace in her hands. Then she looked up. *"Ms. Harbour, I really needed to hear that. Thanks."*

"You're welcome."

"I'm really glad you're my lawyer."

"Trust me, Ms. Davalos, I live for clients like you. Now let's get your affairs in order, shall we?"

Chapter 41

Seba opened the Saved Images folder on his computer and had to admit he'd joined the Blue Shirt Club over the past few days.

He was obsessed.

In his defense, all the pictures he'd downloaded of Vic had him in them, too. And she was always holding his hand in them ... or looking up into his eyes ... or looking at him as he glared at a camera.

His favorite was a gif one of Vic's fans had made of him running up to her in the parking garage. It was two seconds looping over and over of Seba reaching out to cup Vic's chin while she looked up at him like ... exactly how he wanted to be looked at.

At least, by her.

Even in profile on a cell phone camera filming from a safe distance, the look got to him.

He still remembered how strong the instinct had been to kiss her. Had nine men not been in his blind spot with the intent to kill, he might have. But he'd been pretty invested in making sure she didn't die at the time.

Man, what a ride they'd been on together. It had certainly thrown Seba's world for a loop. Personally and professionally.

From Thursday through Sunday, his reputation had gone through a shredder to the point that The Broker suspended his account, pending review.

But the second the sun rose on Monday, he'd never been more in demand.

After Vic's lawyer had settled everything with her, apparently, she'd sent out corrected balance sheets to every person Evan Bauer had ever worked with. The man was being sued into the ground and had fled the country.

On the dark web, people saw Seba as part of the takedown and it was raining offers. Those who weren't offering for jobs, offered gifts and vacations.

He'd messaged no one back and accepted no offers, even though they all led down a path he'd thought he wanted when he'd moved to L.A..

A path to power. A path to influence. A path to wealth.

To take on the big boys, Seba had to be one of the big boys. That's what he'd told himself. But after three days with Vic, he wasn't so sure.

He wasn't sure about much anymore. Even Vic.

She was back.

She'd been back in L.A. for three days—three days, and she hadn't reached out once. She hadn't even tried.

Word was, she was buying a house up in the Hills with a killer view.

She'd also put out a press release stating that Vic Davalos was no more and set up a countdown clock on her website counting down to introducing the world to the new her. It would zero out in two days.

On Saturday, at 6:00 p.m..

Seba was certain that wasn't a coincidence.

But she hadn't reached out.

True, she didn't know where he lived and she didn't have his number, but all she had to do was send up a flare, light some shoes on fire, or whatever, and he would be there.

She hadn't.

At least she had good security now. He'd checked.

In odd moments, it occurred to him that she might not reach out. Ever. He might be part of a memory she wanted to bury forever, now that she'd had the time and space to think about it properly.

That's when he started looking at pictures and telling himself she needed time. The connection they had was way too deep to walk away from without a word.

She'd reach out to him when she was ready. Then he'd kiss her so she really had something to think about before walking away after everything they'd been through. Seba didn't know what was next for him, but he knew it didn't involve walking away. It didn't involve accepting any of those invitations for vacations and swanky parties while he waited, either.

If he heard Vic was doing something like that when she could have been with him, it would tear his heart out. So he couldn't do it to her.

All he could do was exactly what he said he would: wait. And while he wasn't proud of his internet-gleaned photo album, the pictures were a great reminder that what he was waiting for wasn't a figment of his imagination.

Vic had really looked at him like that. A *lot.*

And life wouldn't be right until she was looking up at him like that again … like she looked in the two-second gif that had Seba slamming his laptop shut when he watched it enough times to grow frustrated with himself.

Man, he should have kissed her. If he'd kissed her, she would have been on his doorstep three days ago—the moment she flew in. She would have gotten his address from that Pimpernel guy, and she would come straight his way from the airport.

But he hadn't kissed her. And she hadn't run to him straight from the airport. And life was hell now as he once again counted down to Saturday at 6:00 for the second week in a row. Although, this time, he knew what he was counting down to: Ria's debut fashion show.

Vic hadn't announced she was Ria yet, but that was the name of the fashion show he had tickets for and Seba hadn't forgotten the dream she'd shared in the dark.

Vic-to-Ria.

She was doing it and Seba was going.

He wasn't sure who he was going to show up as yet. He wasn't sure if she wanted to see him, or if his presence would steal her thunder, but he had to be there to see her launch her dream.

While he was at it, he should probably revisit his own dreams because the one that had brought him to L.A. sucked. Seba was done working for other men. He needed to find his own vision. It had gotten lost in the mix somewhere over the years, and only tickled back to life while helping Vic.

He wanted more of that.

Glancing over at the book Isa had gifted him, Seba debated paying the woman another visit. He had a few more questions for her after reading it and he knew the *abuelas* would be more than happy to feed him again while getting gossip and updates.

He just knew they'd all ask about Vic, and he wasn't ready to answer those questions yet.

Rubbing his hands over his hair, Seba looked at the clock.

It was 4:14 in the afternoon and he was sitting on his butt at home.

What a winner.

Maybe he should go to the gym again. Staying in shape was the only thing that felt right at this point. Everything else felt like a waste of time.

Knock, knock.

The sound came from the door in his apartment, and Seba's heart skipped a beat.

He wasn't expecting a package. He was hoping for something—rather, some*one*—else, but told himself to keep expectations in check as he stepped through the wardrobe and closed it behind him. Then he went to the door, flipped all the locks, and pulled the door open to find spiky, blonde hair framing a face he knew better than any other.

Vic's eyes were bright. Clear. Happy. And maybe a little nervous as she looked up at him wearing a feminine take on a man's suit—no tie, and top two buttons unbuttoned on her shirt.

The hair was different. Way different. But the short, new style gave him a clearer view of her cheeks and adorable ears and, oh, man, her neck.

She had an amazing neck.

When she bit her bottom lip lightly and sent him a shy smile, Seba nearly lost his balance.

"Hey," she softly.

"Hey," he echoed, incapable of anything more as he processed the fact that she'd found him. She was there—right in front of him—everything about her different from what he remembered while still looking like everything he ever wanted.

She seemed to sense his appraisal and a nervous hand came up to fidget with her lapel.

"Different, right?" she said.

"Different," he breathed, taking in the details and fighting the urge to thread his fingers through her hair to feel if it was as soft as it looked. "But really good."

That earned him a light blush. "Can I, uh, come in?"

Seeing her off balance gave him his footing back.

"Of course," he said, opening the door wide. "How did you find me?"

She smiled. "You wouldn't believe it, but a psychic actually stopped me on the street at lunch." She pulled a piece of paper out of her pocket and handed it to him. "She handed this to me and was, like, *'Girl, stop playing stoic. You know there's only one place you want to be right now.'* Then she walked off."

Seba unfolded the paper and found his address written on it. Next to it was a heart with an arrow drawn through it.

It wasn't any less weird than a letter with a blue flower on it so Seba decided not to question it. "How do you know she's a psychic?"

"Oh, she's pretty famous," Vic replied, taking note of his barren apartment with a pinch of confusion between her brows. "Super pricey, too. I think I heard someone say they paid her $5,000 for an hour once."

"Whoa," Seba said, handing the paper back. "And she does freebies like this on the side?"

Vic's grin was ironic as she took the paper back, making sure their fingers brushed when she did. Seba felt the tingles of the contact all the way up into his scalp. "I guess."

Oh, man. He was in trouble. One look, one touch, two random words, and he was done. He forgot how to breathe as he searched her eyes to see if she was feeling it, too.

He found his answer quickly. It was a yes, but she was still holding back for some reason.

He pulled his hand away and she cleared her throat.

"I have to say," she said, looking around again. "This is not the grifter lair I was expecting from a guy who gets paid six-figures for three days of work."

Seba played along. "Well, I'm a simple guy."

She arched a brow at him. "I heard a rumor that you're some master at making forgeries. I was kind of expecting displays or something."

It amazed Seba how easy it was to walk over to the wardrobe and reveal the passage to the other side. He'd never shown anyone before, but he didn't even hesitate with her.

"Right this way, my lady."

Her mouth formed a cute little *oh* as she watched the portal open and the smile that followed made everything worth it.

"Now *this* is more like what I was expecting," she said, moving to enter the room without hesitation.

He followed in behind her. "It's more of a workspace. I store things elsewhere so anything here is a work in progress."

"Oh. My. Gosh," she said, looking around. "Your clothes!"

"I know," he said. "I've got a lot."

She sent him a narrow look. "For all your personalities?"

He nodded. "Gotta dress for the job."

"Mmhmm." She didn't sound happy about that, but didn't elaborate either. "Show me something you made."

"Well, the big stuff is in storage," he said, trying not to sound like he was bragging, even though he definitely was. "Here, I mainly have jewelry and accessories. What would you like to see?"

She looked as excited as he'd ever seen her. "What's the last thing you made?"

"A coin," he said, pointing toward his sanding belt. "It's actually not done yet. Work in progress."

"Let's see," she said with enthusiasm.

Just like that, Seba felt like a little kid all over again— eager to share his most recent drawing and hear someone moon over it.

Man, he was so gone on this woman. If it didn't feel so good, he'd feel like an idiot for how much he glowed when her jaw dropped as she accepted the newly rounded coin from him.

"Are you serious?" she said, turning it over in her hand and running her thumb over the curve. All it needed was a little bit of aging added and it would be done. "You made this?"

"Well, a machine did a lot of the work this time around, but yes. That is a forgery."

She looked up at him, jaw dropped. "You weren't kidding. You really could sell forgeries like this."

Seba couldn't help it. He smirked. "All day long, babe."

She blinked at the 'babe' part and Seba almost felt like

apologizing until he saw her blush. Then she bit her lip and handed the coin back.

"Think you'll ever really do anything like that?" she asked. "Open a gallery? Do something legit?"

He felt himself bristle a bit. "Oh, I'm legit."

She looked up at him, blue eyes looking into his soul as she said, "Prove it."

It felt like a slap.

"Excuse me?"

She dropped her gaze, putting a little bit of distance between them. "Here's the thing, Seba. I've had a little time to think about us—"

Us. He liked where her head was at.

"I'm launching my dream this Saturday, thanks to a lawyer who knows how to move mountains. And every time I imagine it, I can't see it without you." She met his eyes again, this time with a little pleading. "I want you there. I want to walk the press line with you. I want you to be my date and to celebrate with you after the show, but I only want it on one condition."

Seba felt himself come into a heated focus as he braced for what came next. "What condition is that?"

Her smile was shy and she had a dreamy look in her eye that almost made him lose it as she said, "I want you to show up as you. I want Sebastian Kahn to show up for me Saturday, and every day after."

Then she broke eye contact again and started pacing.

"I've had a chance to become familiar with some of your alter-egos, and when I'm with you, I don't want Brock Carter to show up ... or Allan Ellis ... and I *definitely* don't want to meet Kaden Salomon or any personas you have like him." She stopped pacing. "I want you. If we give us a shot, I need the real Sebastian Kahn, and I want the con gone."

Seba's heart found a new beat at her request. Steady, yet uncertain; determined, yet terrified.

Vic wanted him to show up as himself? The person he'd

been running away from since he started hiding from Child Protective Services when he was twelve?

Who was Sebastian Kahn, if not the guy who was whoever he needed to be to get by?

Vic reached into the breast pocket of her jacket and pulled out a ticket. It had the same bright-blue iris logo on it as the ticket he already had.

Seba had recognized it the first time he saw it. For some reason, Vic had made her new logo the spitting image of Hoodie Girl's eyes. It was an odd choice for a clothing line, but striking. He wanted to ask her about it.

Another time, though.

Vic held the ticket out to him. "Here's a ticket to my show. Front row. I hope you come. I'd love to go out with you after."

Seba took the ticket without a word—being careful *not* to brush skin. Then he stepped in to test the waters.

Vic grew still at his close proximity and swallowed. When he stepped in again, she looked up at him expectantly.

Oh, yeah. There it was. The look.

The look he'd been telling himself he hadn't imagined was still there and looking up at him with parted lips.

He felt a little breathless, too. The air between them felt supercharged with untapped potential. If someone had told Seba he was glowing in that moment, he would have believed them.

He was glowing, she was staring at his lips, and there seemed to be only one thing left to do.

When he leaned in, Vic tipped her chin up, her eyes drifting closed as she more than met him half-way. There was a moment where their breath crossed streams and she grew still for a beat before pushing up on her toes.

Seba dodged her lips at the last moment and brought his mouth around to her ear. "See you Saturday at 6:00."

She froze in surprise at the dodged kiss, then pressed her hands to his chest and pushed him away. "Are you kidding me?"

"Guess you'll have to wait to see if you want to kiss whoever shows up on Saturday."

She slapped his arm. "You're so mean!"

He laughed. He couldn't help it. Now that he knew he had her, he could wait a few days and do things right. In the meantime, he'd let her wait just like he had.

"Me? Who had to find out you were back in town from a press release?"

Guilt flashed in her eyes, but her chin went up. "I was figuring out what I wanted!"

Seba pursed his lips with playful skepticism and started back for the apartment. "And it took you three days and a psychic to get to me on that list?"

She chased after him. "You *know* that isn't how it is!"

He shrugged before stepping through to the other side. "Well, maybe I need a few days to figure out what I want, too."

"Oh, please!" she scoffed, following him through. "We've both seen the pictures. You're so into me."

"Really?" he said, heading to the front door. "Because when I look at the pictures, it looks like you're the one who's into me."

She grinned like she'd won. "That's because you're only looking at me, babe."

Oh, she almost had him with that one. No one had called him "babe" in his life and he would have thought he'd hate the term aimed his way.

He didn't.

His knees actually buckled a little and his hand twitched with the need to reach out and prove to her she was right.

But he reached for the doorknob instead.

"I guess we'll see who's looking at who on Saturday."

"Hmm," she said, brushing past him as she moved to the door. He shivered at the contact and it made her next words smug. "I guess we will."

Now she was the one teasing, but he didn't mind one bit. She could tease and tempt him all she wanted, but he wouldn't have the tale of their first kiss be one where she showed up and found him moping in his gym clothes and he just went for it.

Not a chance.

Seba might not know exactly who he was, but he wasn't *that* guy.

Vic deserved to be swept off her feet, so that's exactly what he'd do.

"Don't worry about picking me up," she said as she stepped out in the hall. "I'll be at the venue all day."

He leaned against the door frame. "Plan on going out after."

"Oh, I will," she said, playing coy again. "But know I have high expectations. I've pretty much been waiting for this runway show my whole life."

He raised a brow. "You've been waiting for the *runway show*, huh?"

She grinned wide, humor in her eyes. "Yeah. The runway show. It's what I've dreamed of. Only better."

He was grinning like a fool right back. "Well, trust me. The wait's going to be worth it."

She threw her head back and laughed. "You are so full of yourself."

"Nah," he said, shaking his head. "I just know what I'm willing to do for you. See you Saturday."

Then he shut the door and leaned against it—smiling like a fool as he counted slowly to seven before hearing her let out a light huff of frustration and start down the hall.

Then he pushed away from the door himself and headed to his workroom. It was time to start planning for Saturday.

Chapter 42

From a door cam across the street from Seba's apartment complex, Jack and Kali had a clear view of Vic as she exited his building and took a moment to lean against the door and sigh.

"Looks like the reunion went well," Kali said with a smile.

Vic—or maybe Jack should start calling her Ria now—straightened and did a little jig on the stoop before skipping down the steps to where a town car awaited her.

"I think they're going to be okay," Jack agreed.

Kali nodded and Jack looked her way.

"How does Mrs. Hyper-Private feel about someone turning her iris into a name-brand logo?"

Kali shrugged. "A creepy button on your clothes is better than a bad tattoo, I guess. But she's putting way too much stock in what I did."

"You saved her life."

"Well, yeah," Kali conceded dismissively. "But you were the one juggling a hundred mirrors without anyone noticing. I just kept a few from dropping."

Jack had to admit that he surprised himself on this one. He, Ace, and Kali had made a great team.

"Besides," Kali added. "Did you see how she handled Ceravene? That woman is her own spirit animal. She should have her own iris as her logo."

Jack nodded his agreement. "Yes, but sometimes it's easier to look outside for inspiration."

"Hmm. Yeah. I guess I get that."

The signature percussion of a helicopter approaching pulled Jack's eyes toward the Vegas landscape.

"Three guesses as to who that is," he said.

"Landing on the roof this time," Kali mused. "Margot's in a good mood lately."

Yes. She was. When Jack had informed her they would be catching Ceravene about twenty-four hours before it happened, it looked like a fifty-pound backpack had dropped off Margot's back.

"Let me know when it's done," was all she had said. It's all she could say, but this win meant as much to her as it did to him. Maybe, even more. Jack could feel it.

On the screen, the town car drove off just as the helicopter landed above. Both he and Kali turned and waited for the elevator to ding. It didn't take long.

"Well, I think our work here is done," Wanda said, breezing out of the elevator when the doors slid open. She had her hair up in a jumbo braid bun this time, and wore a bright yellow pencil dress with a long royal blue jacket.

The woman had to be burning up in the Vegas heat, but she wasn't letting it show. She never did.

"Right," Kali said."Is this the part where Cupid says, *'And they all lived happily after'*?"

Wanda pulled a face. "Girl, I'd never say that. We all know marriage is a ride, and it ain't all happy."

For a split second, Kali got a faraway look in her eyes, then swapped it out for a smile. "Fair enough."

"And the greater the potential of two soulmates, the tougher their ride to the other side. So, nah, I don't say happily ever after," Wanda said, raising a pointed finger. "I prefer to say, '*And they went their way and raised beautiful babies, who were wise as they were kind, while living worthy of their station'*."

Kali nodded. "I like that."

"That's because it's good," Wanda said, dabbing her finger Kali's way while sending her a little wink. "And, I have to admit, I was a bit iffy about you out of the gate, girl. But you grew on me."

"Uh, thanks?" Kali said, looking amused.

"You *should* thank me," Wanda said, looking Kali up and down. "Because I'm about to help you *so* much. After what you did for my baby, Seba, and his soulmate, I owe you a solid."

Jack held up his hand and stepped in. "She can't—"

Wanda held up her hand right back at him while keeping her focus on Kali. "And I know you're rolling with the Royals right now and you can't accept debts, marks, coins, or favors. But I'm telling you, one day you're going to need a Heart on your side. And when that day comes, remember, I owe you a solid. Prepaid." She turned to Jack, pursing her lips as she looked him up and down. "You, too, if you ever decide to level-up."

"That won't be happening," Jack said firmly.

Wanda smirked as if she thought otherwise, then switched moods.

She jerked her thumb Kali's direction. "Anyway, I'm here to see if I can take this girl to lunch. Because I think we both know she needs a little help with her new identity."

Kali shrugged, clearly indifferent. "I'm fine with it."

Wanda rolled her eyes and turned to face Kali again. "Oh, please, girl. Jack here has you born on the longest night of the year, but that doesn't stop you from walking around like you were born on the hottest day. And look at your hair" — she drew a little circle in the air around Kali's head— "and that face. I still say you have Leo written all over you." She squinted and leaned in. "And those eyes are definitely

Scorpio rising."

Kali's lips parted in surprise and she sent Jack a concerned glance, as if asking if he'd told anyone.

Jack gave a small shake of his head.

But Wanda wasn't done. "I guess you don't have to change anything if you plan on living in the shade the rest of your life. But if you want to talk to people outside of this building or wear anything other than that hoodie for the rest of your life, you've gotta go full Sagittarius, girl. Or people like me are going to take one look at your fake ID and call you out."

Jack and Wanda may not agree on everything, but it felt good to see Kali shell-shocked for once.

Maybe a little bit of Wanda was what Kali needed.

"This is a one-time offer," Wanda added. "Take it, or leave it. But remember what I said. People like me see what you want to hide first. So you need to learn how to hide everything in plain sight while embracing your inner-Sagittarius. Be that perky frat girl who squeals at everything that sparkles, and no one'll see you coming."

Kali rolled her eyes. "I seriously hate frat girls."

"I know. They're the archenemy to your Leo-Scorp pride," Wanda said with a little wave. "But take that up with Jack. He's the one who made your new birth certificate. So you're stuck now."

Kali actually threw her head back and groaned. It was the most childish thing he'd seen her do.

"Fine. Let's do this," she said when she regained her composure. "I'd love to hear your thoughts."

"Perfect!" Wanda chirped before turning to Jack. "You may join us, too, if you don't trust me alone with your Shade."

"I trust you both just fine," he said, jerking his thumb toward his workspace. "Besides, I have a bookcase to finish."

Wanda grinned broadly. "Yes. You should finish that now ... while you have time."

While he had time?

Jack raised his eyebrow in question at her phrasing and was answered with lips pressed together in a secret smile. "I mean, I'd tell you something's coming, but you wouldn't believe me anyway."

Then she sent him a little wink and gestured toward the elevator while looking at Kali. "Shall we?"

"Let's do this."

"Excellent!" Wanda beamed. "First stop, wardrobe!"

Jack smiled and went to go finish Claire's bookcase.

PRATT

Find more books by Sheralyn Pratt
on Amazon.com.

Award-winning rom-com

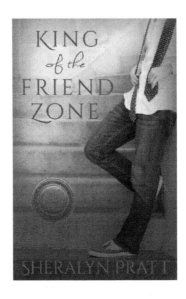

Sheralyn Pratt graduated from the University of Utah with a BA in Communication. A gypsy at heart, she enjoys traveling and acquiring new skills. These days she can nearly always be found out and about with her dog, who has spent hundreds hours watching her type.

She isn't always the best at social media, but loves to connect with readers. Check her out online to see if she's found her groove or still wrestling with the digital world.

Visit Sheralyn online at www.SheralynPratt.com.

Claire — Pimpernel's wife
Pimpernel = JACK
Shade = Kali = partner
Margot =⟩
Wanda =⟩ Psychics ⟨Queen
⟨Cupids - Royals
Seba = Sebastian → hunter
Vic Davalos = Victim Archer, 310
Starbreaker = Assisians
Cerevene = Murder Hired
Ace = A I for Jack
Bauer = Vic's Family
NORA = Vic's Manager
Ryan, Tristan, Chloe, Bret - BodyGuard
DHack - Computer Expert for Seba